Digger Cha... ...e Cops . . .

Lt. Marvin Mannion looked as if he had been up all night. There were deep bags under his eyes, and a faint stubble was showing around his jowls.

"Sit down there," he growled as Digger entered his office. "Do you know a Randy Batchelor?"

Digger sat down.

"What's this all about?"

"I'll ask the questions," Mannion said.

"Good. You answer them, too."

"I can arrest you, you know."

"And I can get sprung in three minutes and you can hold your hand on your ass waiting for answers. What do you think insurance companies do, anyway, with all the money we steal? We hire smart lawyers. So listen, I haven't had much sleep and spending my morning with you isn't high on my list of must-dos, so why don't we be civil and you tell me what this is all about and I'll tell you anything I know."

Mannion thought the offer over.

"You're a brazen bastard, you know," he told Digger.

Books by Warren Murphy

Fool's Flight
Smoked Out

Published by POCKET BOOKS

DIGGER

FOOL'S FLIGHT

#2

WARREN MURPHY

PUBLISHED BY POCKET BOOKS NEW YORK

Another *Original* publication of POCKET BOOKS

POCKET BOOKS, a Simon & Schuster division of
GULF & WESTERN CORPORATION
1230 Avenue of the Americas, New York, N.Y. 10020

ISBN: 0-671-42611-7

First Pocket Books printing February, 1982

10 9 8 7 6 5 4 3 2 1

POCKET and colophon are trademarks of Simon & Schuster.

Printed in the U.S.A.

FOOL'S FLIGHT

BULLETIN

Special to Fort Lauderdale Bugle

FORT LAUDERDALE—Forty-one people, including forty members of a local church heading for a religious retreat in Puerto Rico, are missing in what is presumed to be the crash of their small commercial plane in the Atlantic Ocean.

The chartered flight took off at 9:15 P.M. last night from International Airport, headed for San Juan. Aboard, in addition to pilot Steven Donnelly, were forty members of The Church of the Unvarnished Truth, a fundamentalist mission church in Fort Lauderdale. The forty were on their way to a week-long religious seminar in the hills of Puerto Rico.

But soon after takeoff, the airport lost radio contact with the plane. It was supposed to land in San Juan at around 11:30 P.M. but did not arrive.

What happened to the plane is not known, but Timothy Baker, president of Interworld Airways, said, "We have to fear the worst. No one has seen the plane and it has not landed anywhere."

Coast Guard and Navy aircraft will begin searching the sea along the plane's projected flight path looking for wreckage or survivors.

Chapter One

There should have been a couple of drunks uncon-
scious on the floor and maybe a hooker sitting at a
table, sucking her thumb and making diseased eyes
at any man who came through the door. Instead
there were just these two old rumdums in the tavern,
sitting around the far corner of the L-shaped bar,
arguing.

So Julian Burroughs was annoyed. He stopped
just inside the door of the tavern to listen to what the
two customers were arguing about.

"What do you mean, 'interview ended'?" said
one of them. He wore a cable-knit sweater despite
New York City's summer heat. His face was geneti-
cally red.

The second man wore a blue chambray workshirt
and a felt hat with sweat stains around the band. He
stared down at his drink as if expecting it to flee.

"Interview ended," he said tonelessly.

"You don't say interview ended to me. I ain't
somebody you say interview ended to. Am I,
Freddy?" The man in the sweater looked at the
bartender who was sitting on a stool, reading a
newspaper, guarding his cash register. The bartender looked up in bored annoyance, stared at the man
in the sweater and without any glimmer of interest,
looked back at his newspaper.

"See? If you don't wanna talk to me, you just

don't talk to me. You just don't say interview ended."

"Interview ended," the man in the hat said again.

Julian Burroughs shook his head in disgust, walked the length of the bar, passing up a dozen empty stools, and took the seat directly between the two men. They both turned to look at him and the man in the sweater said, "What do *you* think? You hear what he said to me? What do you think of that?"

"What do I think?" Burroughs said. "What I think is that this place needs a hooker at a table. It needs classier drunks than just you two. You're hardly enough to give the place any real character and I've got a big business meeting scheduled here. I wanted to impress my boss but this place just isn't tacky enough for that. Nothing's any good in New York City these days. I wish the two of you would shut up. That's what I think. Interview ended."

He asked the bartender for vodka on the rocks.

The man in the sweater said, "What do you . . . ?"

Julian Burroughs raised his right index finger for silence and shook his head. "Don't say it, pal, or this interview will really be ended."

The bartender said, "Ernie, you come down here." He picked up Ernie's beer glass and moved it down to the middle of the bar. Ernie followed it as if it were the magnetic north pole and he were an iron filing.

"Don't move him too far away," Burroughs said. "The farther away he gets, the braver he's going to get and the more he's going to talk. I'm not really at the top of my form but if he lips off too much I'm going to have to cancel his reservation."

The man with the hat, on Julian Burroughs' right, was silently watching this conversation. Burroughs took a ten-dollar bill from his wallet and put it on the bar in front of him, as Freddy poured bar vodka into a rocks glass.

"Ernie's a pain in the ass," the man in the hat said.

Burroughs said, "I liked you better when you didn't ad-lib. Go sit over there." He pointed to the corner of the bar against the wall, three stools away. The man in the hat moved.

Freddy turned to replace the vodka on the shelf behind the bar, but Burroughs already had drained his drink and said, "Do it again, Freddy."

Walter Brackler, vice-president for claims of the Brokers' Surety Life Insurance Company, stood inside the doorway, as if unsure whether to step farther into the tavern, run away, or issue an urgent appeal to the Board of Health. Julian Burroughs saw him and waved to him.

"Come on in, Kwash," he called. "There's plenty of room here. My friends here, Sweater and Hat, moved just to make room for you."

Brackler walked the length of the bar and climbed onto a stool next to Burroughs. He was a small man, barely five feet tall, and his face was sour and wrinkled as if his mother had been a lemon and he had been weaned on citric acid.

"Nice place you bring me to, Digger," he said. "Just once, couldn't we meet in the office?" He ordered club soda.

"Ahh, anybody can meet in the office," Digger said. "I think you can always get more done in a bar."

"You seem to have gotten a lot done already."

"You mean I'm drinking too much?"

"You always drink too much."

"The infinite variety of the human species, Kwash."

"Don't get started," Brackler said.

"I suppose you're going to ruin the great charm of this place by trying to insinuate work into it," Digger said.

"Read this." Brackler pushed a newspaper clipping toward him. Freddy turned with the club soda and Brackler turned the glass around in his hand, apparently examining it for cracks and dirt, before he sipped the drink.

After Digger read the clipping, he said, "Too bad. But at least they died in a state of grace, on their way to a religious retreat. Right now their immortal souls are with Jesus."

"And their mortal insurance is with Brokers' Surety Life Insurance Company," Brackler said.

"How much?"

"What would you say if I told you six million dollars?"

"Six million? How the hell did you guys wind up writing six million dollars' insurance?"

Brackler shook his head. "You know those airport insurance machines? We just started moving into that. Our luck, everybody on this goddam plane bought insurance from us. I can just see them, putting in their little twelve quarters to buy a hundred and fifty thou of insurance. They must have stood there in a freaking line, buying insurance, trying to bankrupt our freaking company."

"I can understand your being upset, but let's face it, accidents happen. That's why we have insurance companies. What has this got to do with me?"

"They all had the same beneficiary," Brackler

said. "The Reverend Damien Wardell, pastor of The Church of the Unvarnished Truth. What kind of name is that for a church? He's going to get the six million."

"Now that's interesting," Digger said. "What do you think happened?"

"I don't know. But for six million dollars, somebody might have planted a bomb on that freaking plane."

"My ex-wife would plant a bomb on my plane for free," Digger said.

"She's in good company. Anyway, Mister Stevens thinks a six-million-dollar claim should be looked into. So do I."

"Look," Digger said, "there were forty people on that plane plus a pilot. Cut me a break. It'll take forever to check that out."

"You've got time."

Digger looked past him toward Sweater who had been trying to eavesdrop on their conversation. He turned away. Digger looked behind him at Hat, who began examining the wall next to his seat.

"Do you know it's a proven fact that everybody in the world has five people who want to kill them?" Digger said.

"I . . ."

"You've probably got more than five, but I don't. Only my ex-wife. Maybe my kids, What's-his-name and the girl. The wife has poisoned their minds against me, but I don't think they're dangerous yet. Five potential killers for everybody in the world. Now with forty-one people on that plane, that means . . . forty-one times five . . . two hundred and five potential murderers that have to be checked out. That's an awful lot."

"The entire claims division is at your disposal.

We've got a lot of people working for us. Take what you need."

"No, thank you. If I have to do it, I'd rather do it myself. I've seen your investigative staff. They couldn't find a bull moose in a bathtub. I'll bring my own help."

"You're not bringing that girl, are you?"

"Yes."

"She's a blackjack dealer, for Christ's sakes."

"A good one, too."

"She's Japanese."

"Do you think this plane crash is a Nipponese plot? Besides, she's half-Italian. Actually," Digger said, "she might not want to help us. Insurance work is a comedown for her."

"Do what you want to do. Just do it."

"You say everybody on the plane had insurance?"

"Yeah. Well, everybody but one. Cheap bastard, probably couldn't find the twelve quarters to dump in the machine to gouge us."

"Pilot have insurance, too?"

"Yes. Another one of our airport policies."

"Who was his beneficiary?" Digger asked.

"Reverend Wardell."

"That's inordinately interesting."

"I thought you'd find it so," Brackler said. "Next time, can we meet in the office?"

"Offices are so inhibiting."

"Dammit, Digger, you work for us."

"Only occasionally. And who is us? Actually, I was hired by Frank Stevens, our favorite insurance company president." He crossed himself.

"To my everlasting regret," Brackler said. "I'll tell Mr. Stevens you're working on it."

"And give Frank my love while you're at it."

"Digger, keep the expenses down."

"As long as it doesn't involve my flying Inter-world."

After Brackler left, Digger went to the public telephone and made a credit-card call to the Araby Casino in Las Vegas. When he got the casino manager's office, he said: "I've got a message for Miss Tamiko Fanucci. She's one of your blackjack dealers."

"I'm sorry, sir, but dealers are not allowed to get telephone calls while . . ."

"I know that. Will you please do me a favor?"

"I can't allow . . ."

"Take down this number." Digger read the number off the pay telephone.

"Yes," the woman said.

"When Miss Fanucci gets a break, tell her to call that number. On her *next* break. It's very important."

"This is all very irregular."

"So was my Uncle Mel. Then he started drinking herbal tea. It straightened everything out. He was on the Jewish side of my family. The other side is Irish. They're always regular."

"Excuse me, is your name Digger?"

"Yes."

"Why didn't you say so? I was warned when I first came here that you might call occasionally. I'm supposed to give you anything you want, as long as it doesn't cost the casino any money."

"This won't cost anything. I even paid for the call myself. So you'll tell Koko?"

"Right away."

"Thank you. By the way, how'd you know it was me if you never talked to me before?"

"Mister Needham, the manager, told me how to recognize you."

"How was that?"

"He said you were crazy."

Digger had finished yet another drink when the telephone rang. Sweater started for the phone.

"Don't bother, it's for me," Digger said.

"How's the most beautiful woman in Las Vegas?" he asked.

"You were supposed to call last night," she said.

"Koko, I did call," Digger said.

"You didn't. I was home."

"Okay, then I didn't."

"Where were you?" she asked.

"I don't remember. If I couldn't remember where I was, you couldn't expect me to remember our phone number, could you?"

"Scratch it. What do you want?"

"I want to invite you to go on vacation with me."

"Where?"

"Fort Lauderdale."

"When?"

"Tonight. Think about it. Ocean. Surf. The lap of luxury. All the things you won't see in Las Vegas."

"I just bought two new bathing suits. How long would we stay?"

"How's a week sound?"

"Seven days?"

"It's usually seven days," Digger said.

"I'll buy five more bathing suits."

"Good. Charge them to me," Digger said.

"You don't have a charge account anywhere. Nobody trusts you."

"Then pay for them and I'll give you the money back."

"I don't trust you, either, Digger."

"Good girl. Get the suits and come on down. We both deserve a rest from Vegas."

"I know. I haven't had a real vacation in so long."

"Maybe we'll stay longer than a week," Digger said.

"It would be terrific," Koko said. "This is really nice of you."

"I'm just basically a nice person," Digger said. He looked around the bar. Sweater was shaking his head no. So was Hat.

"No matter what anybody says," Digger said, "I am really a nice person."

Chapter Two

"You prick."

"You're really looking very nice. Is that a new dress? Brown goes with your yellow skin. You look like a very healthy banana."

"You prick."

"Is that anyway to talk to the man who brought you to Fort Lauderdale?"

"No. You're right. You are a pusillanimous, recreant, craven dastard of a prick."

"Dastard's not a noun."

"Yes, it is."

"This is a very unprofessional attitude on your part, Koko."

"I bought seven bikinis. Now I'm supposed to work instead of lying on the beach?"

"You can wear them to bed."

"Bulldookie. I'm wearing chain mail to bed. Armor. Chastity belts. Pull your pudding, you're not touching me."

"I hate it when women use sex to gain their ends," Digger said.

"Nice motel, too. You sure you can afford the eight dollars a day?" She looked around in disgust, then slapped her hand against the ratty blanket on the bed and nodded when a little puff of dust rose from it.

"Everything else is booked up," Digger said.

"We're first on the waiting list at the Howard Johnson's. Listen, stop complaining, I'll work, and you lay around on the beach. How's that?"

"Big deal. Except Fleabag Arms here is sixty miles from the beach. Anyway, you'll start bumbling and stumbling around and I'll wind up doing what I always have to do."

"Which is?"

"Saving your bacon," Koko said.

"I won't need you this time. This whole job's a chipshot."

"Oh?"

"Yes. Only two hundred and five suspects. I proved it to Walter Brackler with infallible Aristotelian logic. He was very impressed and he agreed totally."

"I hate you, Digger."

"As long as you're here, make the most of it. I really wanted you to have a vacation."

"You wanted an unpaid assistant, admit it."

"I don't need you. I'm the expert after all."

"You're nothing without me."

"Oh?" said Digger, as if it were news to him.

"What can you do without me?"

"Light cigarettes in the wind. Women can never light cigarettes in the wind."

"I give up but I hate you anyway."

"Want to make love?"

"Yes, but not to you."

"You'll come around. I'm irresistible."

"I finally know why your ex-wife didn't contest the divorce. What I don't understand is why she just didn't kill you before you left."

"Time out," Digger said. He reached behind him, under his jacket, and through his shirt pressed a button. After a few seconds, he pressed another button. Koko's voice, loud and metallic, filled the small motel

18

room. . . . "pusillanimous, recreant, craven dastard of a prick."

Koko listened for a few more sentences, then clapped her hands over her ears. Digger turned off the tape recorder.

"Must you always wear that thing? Being with you is like a lifetime pass to the filming of 'Candid Camera.'"

Digger patted the tape recorder on his right hip. "The tools of the trade," he said. "I'd be nothing without it."

"You're nothing with it," Koko said.

"That's fair enough," Digger said.

Chapter Three

Tape recording number one, 2:30 A.M. Monday, make that Tuesday, Julian Burroughs in the matter of the Interworld Airlines crash.

I'm talking softly because Koko is sleeping. Or pretending to sleep. Koko, your tits are too small. I hate yellow women, particularly when they think they're smart. You're also lousy in bed and I'm glad you lost World War II.

Okay, she's really asleep but I'll talk softly anyway. There is a simple rule in checking out potential insurance frauds. Get on the tail of the guy who gets rich.

That will be the Reverend Damien Wardell, the pastor of, God help me but it's true, The Church of the Unvarnished Truth.

But there are ways of doing it and ways of doing it. I don't like to go right after somebody frontally. I kind of like to nibble around the edges some and get some background. I think I'll just go and hear one of his sermons first. Maybe I can still be saved.

Brackler has promised the list of victims on the plane crash so soon I'll have names and ages and addresses.

I took Koko for a late dinner tonight. I think she really liked the diner down the road. But she said she wouldn't help me. I'll win her over, though. I'd like to think that's because of my charm, but I don't know. She makes a good part of her living by letting people think they're getting over on her. It's part of her casino's hospitality policy, asking her to be nice to high rollers who suddenly get stricken with yellow fever. Ahhhh, she does what she wants to do and I work for Walter Brackler. So which one's the whore?

I wish my mother liked Koko so I could ask her to explain her to me. Shit. I wish my mother liked *me*. My mother doesn't like anybody, including my father. Maybe she liked Uncle Phil, the only Jewish drunk besides me in the whole world. His liver exploded in the Bronx one day and closed down the George Washington Bridge in both directions for ninety minutes. Shadow Traffic went batshit.

The question of the day: why did that pilot insure himself at some airport machine? Why did he name some hop-in-the-ass preacher as his beneficiary? I read a book once by Bernard Wolfe. One of the chapter headings was "What Ho. Smelling Strangeness."

What ho.

I'll do my expenses tomorrow.

Chapter Four

As Digger turned into the giant parking lot outside the huge white tent, the thought crossed his mind that if God had wanted to be worshipped in tents, he would have made everyone Muslim.

It was nearly 11 A.M. and already the summer sun had hammered Fort Lauderdale into submission.

He slowed down instinctively, looking for a parking lot attendant. Seeing none, he drove on ahead and parked his rented Ford between two pickup trucks. There were four hundred vehicles in the lot, the majority of them campers and pickup trucks with out-of-Florida license plates. No question, Digger thought. The Reverend Damien Wardell was an honest-to-God tourist attraction.

The gravel crunched under his feet and the dust swirled up, talcing the toes of his shoes as he walked toward the tent. It was a giant circus tent but he had never seen a white circus tent before, and it had no scalloping around the sides where the tent roof met the walls. Instead, it seemed to have every intention of being dignified and restrained. And then there was the sign over the entrance. He had heard it but he hadn't really believed it. But there it was. The name of Wardell's church.

CHURCH OF THE UNVARNISHED TRUTH
Reverend Damien Wardell, Pastor

Services: Wednesday, 11 A.M.
Saturday, 7:30 P.M.
Sunday, 11 A.M. and 8 P.M.

Digger stepped up into a family group, father and mother who could be differentiated because he was wearing the plaid shirt and she the flowered, and three children. Moving in a Trojan wedge, they surrounded Digger and marched him into the tent as if they were taking him to the gallows.

The inside of the tent was set up with wooden bleachers, stacked at a sharp angle, surrounding a rectangular center stage. Most of the bleacher seats were already filled and Digger escaped from his temporary family and moved up a flight of rickety wooden stairs to sit in the very back row, high up near the top of the tent.

It was already baking temperature in the tent and Digger felt like a fresh Idaho potato. People were fanning themselves with newspapers and heavy cardboard fans. Down on the stage he saw a piano, a guitar, and an electric bass. He glanced around and met the eyes of the woman sitting next to him. She seemed equipped to be a finalist in the national lady bicep contest.

"Hi, young fella," she said, with a syrupy drawl.

"Hi there," he said.

"First time?"

"Yup."

"Won't be your last. You're in for something, you really are."

"That's what ah heah," Digger said. "You comin' heah long?"

"Since he started the church. Four and a half years ago. We drives down from Georgia ever' chance we gets. He turned my life around."

Yeah, Digger thought. Before, she used to be fat.

"Ever meet him, this Reverend Wardell?"

"The reverend? Sure. Lots of times. Nothing stuck-up 'bout him either, just a regular person, ceppin' God touched him."

"How come I never see him on television when I go up north?" Digger asked.

"He ain' one of those TV preachers. He's a real preacher." She waved with her hand, a gesture condemning the cathode ray tube, television, the photoelectric effect and television ministries to the same rubbish heap.

The conversation stopped as a man walked out and sat at the piano. He wore a medium-gray three-pieced suit and his hair was cut short enough to make Digger realize that entire years had gone by in his life when he had never seen another man's ears. The piano player was followed by two other men, identically dressed, and then a young blond woman with almost white hair, wearing a mid-calf-length white dress. She came onto the stage up a slight ramp that Digger saw led to another door in the tent's wall. She looked like a snowflake, he thought.

She sat primly on a chair while the second two men picked up the stringed instruments and, upon a nod from the piano player, began to play.

Digger wondered if there was a talent agency that dealt in religious music groups; there probably had to be, there were so many preachers. Were they in the musicians' union? Did they pay union dues? Did they tithe? All right, man, let's get it up. Ten percent for the church, ten percent for the agent, ten percent to the union, ten percent for Southern Comfort, and ten percent for some good Mexican dope. What kind of musicians were they anyway?

The blond singer was okay. She had been given a pure voice that could sing on-key and that was what she did. It was all she did. There were no shadings, no nuances, no vocal tricks or experimentation. She sang each song the way it was written in those music books for chord organ . . . big melody notes, bang, bang, bang, right on the beat. It was really a shame, Digger thought, because the voice might have been exceptional if it had been used, truly used. It was Sarah Vaughan and Ella Fitzgerald and Cleo Laine, never asking a question of the music, just taking it as it came.

The blonde's movements were something else again. She was trim and shapely but she moved around the stage woodenly, heavy footed, without grace of gesture or movement.

The woman with the arms next to Digger leaned over and said, "Isn't she good?"

"Raht," Digger said.

"That's Mother Candace."

"Who's she?"

"The reverend's wife."

Digger looked at the blond chanteuse again. She was tall and had milk-fed baby skin. Her hair was so light that it just had to be dyed; yet somehow it looked natural on her. She gave him the impression of a photograph in a darkroom somewhere, sitting in the developer, with the blacks and the grays not yet punched up by the chemicals.

Digger put her age in the late twenties or early thirties, but there really wasn't much way to tell. She had avoided the sun and she did not have the leather-skinned look that he'd seen while driving on the Lauderdale streets, a look that infuriated him because it seemed to testify that its owner, generally a woman, was trying her best to turn into a wallet. Mrs. Wardell was beautiful.

The blonde was through "The Church in the Wildwood," which got a good round of applause and "Rock of Ages," which seemed to be on everyone's top forty because a lot of people hummed or sang along. She got another big hand.

The lights inside the tent dimmed momentarily as one of the musicians knelt over a control box in the far corner of the stage. Then they flared up even brighter and, through loudspeakers all over the tent, a voice sounded.

"God lives. And He *is* King of Kings and He *is* Lord of Hosts and He *is* the Prince of Peace and He's a'coming for all of us, Hallelujah."

The thousand people in the tent echoed "Hallelujah," as if the powerful voice that came over the speakers had issued a command that they could not disobey.

Then, holding a microphone, the Reverend Damien Wardell bounded up the small ramp onto the stage and Digger was disappointed. He had expected a mountain of a man or a prophet with a long beard and hair and fiery black eyes. Instead, Wardell was a small man with a tanned but unlined face. His fine blond hair was long but neat. He wore a white suit with a white shirt and a dark blue tie. His shoes were white.

His face was lean and pinched, but it was a face that seemed without malice. His nose was slightly hooked and his lips were a thin line like a knife slit through raw dough, but he gave the impression of openness and happiness. Perhaps it was his blue eyes. Though they were close together, there were laugh wrinkles at the corners setting them off, opening up his face.

And there was the voice.

It filled the tent, seeming almost to make it

vibrate, and the people in the audience visibly edged forward in their seats, to make sure they did not miss a word.

"The Lord told us: He that believeth on the Son shall hath everlasting life, and he that believeth not the Son shall not see life, but the wrath of God abideth on him.

"You listening to me? He that believeth not the Son shall not see life. But he that believeth on the Son hath everlasting life. If you believe, you live.

"Who you think He was talking to? You think He was talking just to me? You think He was talking just to the man who lives in the big house down the street and tells you every Sunday how much he put in the collection plate? You think He was talking only to presidents or kings or captains of industry or the wealthy and the powerful?

"You think that? You better not think that. Because He was talking to us . . . all of us. . . ." Now, as he spoke, Wardell, holding the microphone and swinging the cord expertly out of the way as he moved, marched back and forth along the stage from side to side. The three musicians and Mrs. Wardell sat on chairs at the rear of the stage, watching.

Later Digger would try to re-create Wardell's sermon in his mind, and realized that if he were to try to write it down, it would look like a page from a script, filled with acting directions, with pauses, with capitals for emphasis.

"He was talking to us . . . all of us." Wardell delivered his words in rhythm with his marching steps along the stage. "He was talking to the rich. He was talking to the poor. He was talking to the sick. He was talking to the healthy. He was talking to the sad. He was talking to the happy. He was talking to all of them and He was saying the same thing to all of them. He was saying, Come with Me, and when we get to that Jordan River, we're walking over together to meet My Father, Hallelujah."

Wardell spoke for almost an hour. He could have left his microphone home, so total was the attention that met his words, but instead he used the microphone as an actor's prop.

Eight or ten times, he built his sermon to climaxes, as he marched back and forth the perimeter of the stage, speaking to the crowd that encircled him. Even when his back was to Digger, Digger could feel the preacher's power, could almost see the tension in his muscles from the way his body moved under the white cloth of his suit, now stained a faint gray with the water of perspiration. Sometimes, legs wide apart, like a classic boxer in the ring, he would punch his fist toward the floor for emphasis . . . word, punch, word, punch.

Around the tent, people by the hundreds thrust their right arm into the air over their head, proof that they were witnessing God along with Wardell.

It was a demonstration of raw power. Digger had the feeling that Wardell could have read from the Yellow Pages and turned his congregation to emotional mush.

But there was nothing primitive about Wardell's sermon. Digger listened carefully and it inveighed against all the things he would have expected—sex, liquor, gambling, and loose life in the fast lane. But starting with his opening quotation from Scripture, Wardell had built a tight, logical progression from step to step that was compellingly sensible.

It was the sort of thing that came easy to no one and it showed how hard Wardell worked at what he did and how carefully he prepared.

He talked, he cajoled, he laughed, he scolded, he complimented himself on his preaching, he wept, tears streaming down his cheeks, but it was all the tip of the iceberg, the visible portion of a brilliant sermon that had been created at a desk with paper and pen.

All around Digger, people were rising in response to the minister's exhortation: "Stand up for God. Show Him that you love Him, as He showed you when He gave His Son to wash you in His precious blood."

Digger rose in his seat, too. Wardell asked for the sick to come forward and stand in front of the stage, and as over a hundred persons picked their way slowly through the crowd, he prayed for everyone at the service.

When the lame and the halt were in front of him, he began to walk back and forth before them. "I cannot heal," he said. "Only God can heal. But I am the vessel into which right now He is pouring His power. In God's name, I order those blind eyes to see. I order those deaf ears to be opened. I order weak hearts to be strong and crooked legs to be straight. Out, cancer. I command it in the name of God, Hallelujah. He's with us today, Christians. Do you feel it? Do you feel the power?" Cries of "yes, yes" echoed through the tent and Wardell shouted, fist punching the air, "Hallelujah."

"I'ma telling you, Devil, and we know you, old hoofprint, we know that it's you that causes sickness and we're telling you now that you're getting out of town. You're not hearing from the sick right now. You're not hearing from the weak. You're not hearing from any preacher who isn't as good a man as he ought to be. You're hearing God's voice, pouring up to you from a man's throat, through a thousand throats. You're listening to the Lord of Hosts and He's curing the blind and He's healing the lame and He's fixing up the ill and He's doing it now . . . right now . . . in the name of Blessed Jesus, Hallelujah, I feel the power, do you all feel it?"

All through the tent, voices roared "Hallelujah, we feel it, Hallelujah."

At the stage, the gallery of ill and lame and sightless were nodding their heads, their right fists raised in the air. From behind Digger could see that the shoulders of many of them were rising and falling as they wept, and he thought that it must have been much like this in the early days of Nazi Germany when Hitler, by his voice alone, inflamed crowds into fits of frenzy.

Then, almost abruptly, Wardell said, "Let us pray," and he intoned a quiet, restrained prayer asking for God's blessing on the congregation. As Mrs. Wardell and the three musicians rose for a gospel song, he walked off down the ramp that led outside the tent. Freed from his power, the audience seemed to stretch and then move toward the exits. Digger jumped lightly from the side of the bleachers to the ground and was into the parking lot before it crowded up.

He drove away toward his next call. He was impressed by Reverend Wardell but with a curious feeling that something had not been quite right about the revival service.

Chapter Five

The older boy sat sullenly in front of the television set, a book open in his lap, a half-spilled glass of milk on the hardwood floor. He was neatly brushing cookie crumbs under his shoe, then crushing them into powder with the sole of his foot. By his side were three suction cup-tipped wooden darts. Two others were stuck on the television screen.

The second boy was perhaps two years younger, maybe seven years old. He knelt on the far side of the room over a checkerboard. The men were neatly arranged but the board rested on a large book. Carefully the boy pulled the board off the edge of the book so it balanced precariously. Then he slammed his fist down on the free edge of the board, tipping it over, shooting the checker pieces into the air. Three of them hit the low ceiling, leaving two red marks and a black smudge. "Shit," the boy said. "Motherfucker."

"Nice kids," Digger said to their mother who had just brought him into the house. Mrs. Steve Donnelly was a small, trim woman who had probably just crossed over onto the liar's side of forty. She had a tight little figure, the kind of shape that would never get fat, but would just thicken up as she grew older and some of the turns softened out. She had shiny dark hair, cut short around her face, but it was a little more uncombed than casual. Her smile was easily worth both of her kids, broad, perfect, large white teeth, an easy smile.

Digger had handed the woman his business card at the door. She glanced at it, handed it back, and asked him in. She closed the door behind him and when he turned to her, she was reaching back to pick up her glass from a low Formica-topped table behind the door.

"It's good of you to come, Mr. Burroughs. Can I offer you a drink? I don't generally drink before dinner but, well, the last two weeks . . . I'm sure you understand."

"Of course," Digger said. "I'll have whatever you're having."

"A martini. Vodka," she said.

"Good. But save your vermouth. I'll just have vodka."

"Why don't you come in here and sit down?" she said, pointing to the living room. The two boys stolidly refused to look at him. The crumb-crusher was pouring a little milk into his crumb-powder on the floor. The checker-destroyer was restacking the checker pieces on the board, which was again balanced on the book.

"I'll be right back," the woman said.

She left the room and the two boys immediately turned to Digger.

"Who are you? Are you going to be our father?" the younger one asked.

He had a whiney voice that sounded as if it belonged to someone who would spend his life licking snot from under his nose.

"Christ, I hope not," Digger said softly so that their mother wouldn't hear him.

The younger boy made a face at him and stuck out his tongue. The older beast thumbed his nose.

32

Digger stood up and grabbed his crotch in their direction.

They turned away and Digger sat back down and looked around the room. There was an old upright piano with white water stains from wet glasses on it. The television set was black and white and the picture was two inches shy, top and bottom, of filling the screen. There was a rug that had not been too good to start with but could now be advertised as "worn tan with flecks of tired brown."

Digger had always assumed that airline pilots were reasonably well off, but Mrs. Donnelly, recent widow of Steve Donnelly, chief pilot for Interworld Airways, was not exactly ready to buy a seat on the New York Stock Exchange.

From his seat on the couch, he could see their car out alongside the house. It was a Volvo station wagon, the kind that advertised it would go for hundreds of thousands of miles but missed the point. Americans didn't want cars that went hundreds of thousands of miles under one owner; they wanted a car that shouted every three years, "Hey, folks, I'm a new car, screw you and your Volvo."

The two boys had not looked at Digger since he had made his gesture to them. Their mother came back into the room, holding her martini as if her life depended on it. She handed Digger his drink.

"He grabbed his dick, Mama," the older one sniveled. "He grabbed his dick and waved it at me."

The younger one was busy throwing checker pieces at the ceiling.

Mrs. Donnelly looked at Digger who shrugged his shoulders and looked up at the seven-and-a-half-foot-high ceiling.

"Oh, stop it," Mrs. Donnelly said, as she sat on a chair facing Digger. "It's nice to have company and an excuse to have a drink," she said.

"Sure is," Digger said.

"I don't like him, Mama," the older boy screamed. "He grabbed his dick."

Mrs. Donnelly looked at Digger with a smile of what-can-you-do-with-such-wonderfully-creative-and-imaginative-children? Digger smiled back with a smile that said Try-dipping-them-in-molten-lead-and-using-them-for-doorstops.

"Why don't you children go out and play?" she said, turning to them. Immediately both boys went back to their chosen professions, the older one to crumb-crushing, the younger one to checker-launching.

"Go ahead," she cooed. "Go outside."

"We don' wanna," the older one said.

"Mister Burroughs and I have to talk. Big grown-up things that you won't want to hear."

"You and him is gonna fuck."

Her back still to Digger, she tittered, "Oh, come on, Josh. Go ahead outside."

"No."

The smaller one agreed. "No."

"Get the fuck out. Both of you. *Now!*" Her scream snapped both children from their catatonia. They scrambled to their feet leaving crumbs and milk and checkers behind and ran from the room. A few seconds later, Digger heard the front door slam.

She turned back to Digger and sat in a chair at right angles to the couch where he sat. Their knees were only a few inches apart.

"Hi," she said with forced cheerfulness, then sipped her drink.

"High-spirited boys," Digger said.

"Yes. And wonderful imaginations. They're kind of lost without their father and I just haven't . . . well, I don't have the heart to crack down on them just yet. So soon."

"It has to be a difficult, trying period for them," Digger said.

"Yes. For all of us." She smiled at him with heavily mascaraed lashes.

There was a smell in the room of stale cigarettes and in reaching for the ashtray, Digger looked down at the carpet in front of the couch and saw three small burn holes and a long cigarette burn mark. Mrs. Donnelly would be a lady who'd fall asleep on her couch at night with a cigarette burning in her hand.

"So what can I do for you, Mr. Burroughs?"

"I'm with the claims department of Brokers' Surety Life Insurance Company. Your husband was insured with us and it's usual procedure to check out accidental matters like this."

"I understand. It's funny, when you have insurance and you never think about it, but it gets really important. I bet I couldn't even find the policy, but that insurance will be all we have to live on."

"That's the reason for our industry's existence," Digger said. "To make it possible for people to survive in troubled times. That's what my boss, Walter Brackler, always tells me. He says we're here to serve the American public."

"How long do you think it will be before I get a check?" Mrs. Donnelly said.

"What check?"

"From my husband's insurance."

"You're not the beneficiary."

"What?"

"No. The beneficiary is the Reverend Wardell. He's the pastor of that church," Digger said.

"I know who he is. What the hell are you talking about?"

"Your husband's policy is made out to him."

"In a pig's ass, it is," Mrs. Donnelly said. She

slugged down her drink, got up from the chair and walked from the room. Fifteen seconds later she was back with an insurance policy that she had never even thought of.

"Found it, I see," Digger said.

The woman was standing in front of Digger, reading through the typewritten pages at the back of the policy. She nodded as she found what she was looking for, folded the pages over and handed it to Digger. "There," she said triumphantly.

He looked at it. In the place for beneficiary was written Trini Donnelly, wife. He looked at the front of the policy. It was a fifty-thousand-dollar policy written with Prudential.

"Well?"

"You're the beneficiary of this policy. Of course," Digger said.

The woman sat back down.

"Then what are you talking about?"

"Your husband had another policy. See, this one's with Prudential. I'm with B.S.L.I. Your husband took out one of those airport insurance policies before the accident. He made it out to Reverend Wardell. Why do you think your husband would do that?"

"Steve turned into a Holy Roller. He used to go to that church all the time. You know how dull it is having some psalm-singer hanging around the house masquerading as your husband? You want another drink?"

"Yes."

"Hold on." She went into the kitchen and made two more drinks, then brought them to the living-room door. "Let's sit in the kitchen," she said.

"Okay."

They sat at a round kitchen table on wrought-iron

chairs whose vinyl cushions had lost almost all trace of color.

Mrs. Donnelly seemed to have recaptured her pose as grieving widow, Digger noticed, because she shook her head sadly and said, "Poor Steve."

"Your husband was a member of Wardell's congregation?"

"Congregation? That's a laugh. Wardell's zoo. Faith healing. Clapping their hands. Rolling around on the floor. What bullshit. Yeah, he was a member."

"How long?"

"Last year or so. After he hooked on with that rinkydink airline. This insurance is for fifty thousand?"

Digger looked again at the Prudential policy. There was no double-indemnity provision for accidental death.

"Fifty thousand dollars," he said. "The company bought this for him?"

She nodded. "All the airlines do that. When I was a stew, I always had insurance. And Steve, too. When he was with Pan-Am and American. Mister Burroughs . . ."

"Julian."

"All right, Julian. You just look around you and you can see we're not quite living in the lap of luxury. We haven't even climbed up on its leg yet. Steve couldn't buy a bus ticket. He couldn't afford to pay for insurance. What about Wardell's, how much is that for?"

"If you don't mind my saying, Mrs. Donnelly . . ."

She touched his right hand. "My turn," she said. "Trini."

"Okay. Trini, I always thought that airline pilots

made a lot of money. I'm just . . . well, surprised that things are so tight for you."

"Pilots do make a lot of money. It helps though if you're flying for a real airline and not that barrage balloon outfit Interworld. It helps if you work regular. It helps if you don't have a lot of old drinking and gambling debts to pay off."

"Steve drank?" Digger could feel the woman flinch. Her hand moved away from his. She was thinking that she might have said something that could cost her insurance money. Digger put his hand on hers. "It doesn't matter, Trini. It doesn't have anything to do with the insurance." He smiled at her, reassuringly.

"He didn't drink anymore. He used to. He used to drink everything. He lost his good jobs because of his drinking. Then he got himself sobered up and went to work with Interworld. He didn't drink anymore. He didn't have time. He just went to church or whatever Wardell calls his tent show. I never thought he'd leave money to him, though. I used to think he was just telling me he was going to church and he had a girlfriend stashed somewhere. But I checked and there he was, in church with the other loonies. He'd hang out down there and I guess help them clean the elephant crap out of their tent. How much was the insurance for?"

"Do you have any idea how the accident might have happened?" Digger asked, ignoring her question.

She shrugged and took her hand out from under Digger's to hold her martini with both hands. Her hands were small and her skin was soft.

"It's hard to say. Steve was really a good pilot. Maybe the plane exploded or something. Whatever it was, it wasn't Steve's fault. He was really good, Mr. Burroughs."

"Julian."

"Julian. Steve was really a good pilot, particularly now that he was sobered up. How much was the other insurance for?"

"You didn't really believe he was going to church at first?" Digger said.

"No. Not until I followed him there. Then I thought he was getting it on with that Mrs. Wardell, but when I looked at her, I realized she'd never go for him. She's too cold and formal, and Steve liked his girls bouncy. How much was the other insurance for to Wardell?"

"A quarter of a million."

"Bullshit. I don't believe it."

"It's true."

"I'll sue," she said.

"Sue who?"

"Wardell. That brainwashing bastard. His wife. Somebody. I get a stinking fifty thousand dollars out of all this and that horseshit station wagon out there and two sociopaths for kids and this house with nothing in it and vinyl cushions you can read through and Wardell gets a quarter of a million? For what, for singing 'Rock of Ages'?"

"Maybe your husband wanted him to carry on his work?"

"What work? He's an auctioneer in a robe. I'll fight it in court. I wasn't married all these years so Wardell gets rich when Steve dies. The court'll understand things like that. I'm his wife. Those two are his kids. We deserve that money."

"Of course you do." Digger realized that Trini Donnelly was on the edge of being very drunk.

"When we got married, I never thought it was going to end up like this. I could have married a lot of people. He was a senior captain. What have I got, I got shit."

"Well, anything that I can do . . ."

"What can you do?"

"Nothing, I guess. But you seem to think that Wardell might have done something underhanded to get your husband to sign insurance to him. Maybe that'll check out. If it does, well, we'll see. Maybe something could work out."

"I'm going to sue."

"Just wait a little bit until you see how everything turns out."

"Maybe you're right. Fresh drink?"

"No thanks," Digger said. "I've got a long day's work."

"Would you like to stay for lunch?"

"I don't think your sons would approve."

"Who cares? I can send them over to a neighbor's. Get them lost for a couple of hours. She's got two morons that I watch too."

Digger stood up and held Mrs. Donnelly's hands in his. "If I didn't have work to do, I'd take you up on that offer in a flash."

He squeezed her hands hard. She looked into his eyes trying to make hers limpid. They were a little bloodshot.

"Well, I owe you one. The door is always open," she said.

"I'll be around town a few days. Maybe later, Trini."

"I hope so."

"I can let myself out."

"Okay. If you see my boys, tell them to stay near the house. Unless somebody offers them a chance to run away and join the circus. Tell them to take it."

The two boys were on the curb in front, near Digger's rented car. As he stepped out of the house, he reached behind him and pressed a button turning off the tape recorder that had been running through-out the conversation with Trini Donnelly.

The older boy said to Digger, "Did you fuck?"

"You're a disgusting little creep."

"I'm gonna tell my mama."

"She doesn't want you in that house. She said go play in the street. In the middle. If you ever give me any snot again, I'm going to remove your scrotum. Both of you. Now get the hell out of here."

The two boys ran away and Digger got into his car and drove off, thinking the Donnelly family wasn't exactly the Waltons.

Chapter Six

Digger entered police headquarters and went directly to the basement because detective bureaus were
always in the basement.

A policeman in plainclothes sat at a desk inside
the door. Digger knew he was a policeman because
he was trying to type with two fingers, neither of
which seemed to be able to select one key over
another. He was swearing a lot under his breath.

He looked up, saw Digger and said, "Be with you
in a minute." He hunched forward over the typewriter and raised his right index finger high into the
air. His eyes scanned the keyboard. He seemed to
find what he was looking for. The index finger
crashed down. The policeman shook his head and
sighed. "Yes, sir, what can I do for you?"

"My name's Burroughs. I wanted to see the
detective commander."

"That would be Lieutenant Mannion."

"What'd you say your name was?"

"Burroughs." Digger handed him a business card.

"What is it about, Mr. Burroughs?"

"That plane crash two weeks ago. I'm with the
insurance company."

The plainclothesman nodded and dialed two digits
on his phone.

"An insurance guy named Burroughs is here
about that plane crash." He nodded and put his

hand over the mouthpiece. "He says what about that plane crash," he told Digger.

Digger shrugged. "I'm looking into it. This is kind of a courtesy call."

"It's kind of a courtesy call, Lieutenant," the officer reported dutifully. He listened some more, then hung up. "He said he's too busy right now to be courteous."

Digger got up. "Okay. Hang onto my card for him, though, will you?"

"Sure thing."

Digger had his hand on the doorknob when he heard a voice bellow behind him.

"Burroughs."

He turned around to see a man shaped roughly like a refrigerator standing in the door to one of the side offices.

"Yeah?"

"I'm Mannion. Come on in but be quick about it."

Digger followed Mannion inside. If Hollywood had been casting about for a cop to play Broderick Crawford, instead of always the other way around, Mannion would have been a natural. He was big and square. His hair was thinning on top and his voice had an echo, almost as if it rattled around inside the massive body before finally escaping from the mouth. Mannion had bags under his eyes and big puffy jowls that made him look vaguely like an orangutan.

"What do you want?" Mannion asked. He sat behind his desk but didn't invite Digger to sit. Digger sat anyway.

Digger fished another business card from his wallet, checking first to make sure it carried his real name.

"I'm Julian Burroughs, with Brokers' Surety Life Insurance Company." He handed Mannion the card. The policeman looked at it, then dropped it in the wastepaper basket alongside his desk.

"That won't stop me," Digger said. "There's more where that came from. My printing budget is unlimited."

"What kind of a name is Burroughs?"

"Two syllables, nine letters, your usual kind of name."

"That's not what I mean. You know what I mean."

"It's Irish."

"You Irish?"

"My father's Irish," Digger said.

"You're not?"

"I'm half-Irish."

"What's the other half?"

"Jewish."

"You Catholic or Jewish?"

"Neither."

"You an atheist?"

"I'm a born-again drunk."

Mannion looked at him as if he were a gravy stain on a favorite tie. Finally, he said, "What do you want here anyway?"

"My company had insurance on that plane that went down a couple of weeks ago. I'm looking into it."

"What for?"

"Before we pay. Just a normal check. I just wanted to stop in and let you know I was in town."

"You always do that?"

"I try to. I think it's a good idea. If my name comes up for any reason, you'll know who I am."

"If your name comes up for any reason, it'll mean that you broke the law and if you break the law, I'll arrest your ass."

"You know, Lieutenant Mannion, I get this idea that you don't like me."

Mannion's big hands clenched and unclenched. Why would he want to hit me, Digger wondered. The big policeman leaned back in his chair and said, "You are right. Now I guess we understand each other."

"I guess we do."

"What are you going to be looking into?"

"Survivors of everybody dead on the plane. Beneficiaries. Things like that. You know anything about Reverend Damien Wardell?"

"Nothing bad. He runs a church. He doesn't cause trouble. He doesn't push shit and he doesn't fence hot stuff. He leaves us alone and we leave him alone. Good advice for some other people to take."

"You know him personally?" Digger asked.

"No. Why, you interested in him?"

"He's going to get some money out of the accident. Any idea what caused the accident?"

"What do I know from planes?" Mannion asked. "Maybe it wasn't an accident. Maybe they all flew away to go drink Kool-Ade in Africa. What do I know? The F-A-whatever the hell it is was in. They do things like that. I don't. Maybe if it crashed on the Galt Ocean Mile, I'd get involved. But it didn't, so I don't."

Mannion sat up straight in his chair, then leaned forward toward Digger. "Listen," he said. "You find out anything and I want to know. If there's anything fishy, I want to know. If something went down that shouldna gone down, I want to know. You got that?"

"You'll be the first one I tell," Digger said. He rose from his chair. "I'll be going now."

"You handle car insurance?" Mannion asked.

"I don't sell insurance."

"I don't mean you. I mean your company."

"Only life insurance."

"Another scam. There ought to be a law against you people."

"There probably is," Digger agreed cheerfully.

"Good, I'm busy," Mannion growled.

"Never too busy to be nice, though," Digger said. "Thanks for seeing me."

He let himself out.

The plainclothesman said, "He's not in a good mood since his car's fender got banged up and the insurance didn't cover it."

Digger looked at the nameplate on the desk. Detective Dave Coley.

"Listen, Detective," he said. "I'm in town to do some checking. Sometimes I can use a local cop. You interested? Do you do private work?"

Coley glanced over his shoulder to make sure Mannion's office door was closed. "Sometimes."

"My company's generous. Got a card?"

Coley fished one out of the desk drawer. He scrawled another number on the back of it.

"That's my home number. If you want me, give me a call. I'm steady days here and most nights I'm home."

"Okay," Digger said. He pocketed the card. "This is just between us," he said.

Dave Coley nodded.

After he left Coley, Digger turned off the tape recorder. The Lauderdale heat slapped him in the face as he stepped outside the police building. He hated Florida. The heat and humidity mugged a person's body. The whole state was fit only for people who spent their days and nights hiding away in air-conditioned bars or air-conditioned movies or were so old they needed incineration to convince themselves they were warm.

The public telephone booth on the corner near headquarters felt like a sauna as he stepped inside. Someday, someone was going to invent a good tape recorder, small enough for him to hide inside his sock, and he wouldn't have to go around wearing a jacket all the time to conceal the giveaway bulge on his right hip.

He dialed his motel number.

"This is Mister Burroughs in Room 317. Any messages for me?"

"No, sir, the box is empty."

"Would you ring my room?"

"Sure. Hold on."

The telephone started ringing but there was no answer. Digger wanted to leave a message with the clerk for Koko but he knew the operator would never come back on the line. Digger could stay plugged into Room 317's line until the telephone rotted in his hand, but the clerk would never come back on the line. Why did they do that?

Why did French designers make shirts with sleeves designed for people with sticks for arms? Why, after he had spent years learning to strike a match with one hand, did somebody decide to put the striker on the backside of the matchbook? Why did Italian bread go stale after just one hour in the refrigerator?

There were so many problems in the world. Why didn't somebody solve them? Did they have to leave them all for him? Did he have to do everybody's job?

Where the hell was Koko? She should have had enough sun by now. He slammed the receiver back onto the hook.

He looked at the phone directory under the shelf of the booth but the pages looked as if they had been the sole sustenance for a family of mice.

From information, he got the number of Interworld Airways, called, and asked to speak to Timothy Baker, identified in his newspaper clipping as the president of the company.

"Mr. Baker's on the other line. Who's calling, please?"

"Never mind."

Digger hung up, satisfied that Baker was in his office. On the way back to his car, he stopped in a liquor store and bought a half-gallon of vodka for his room. For later.

Chapter Seven

The Interworld Airways company was headquartered in a quonset hut at the farthest end of the Fort Lauderdale airport. The building needed a paint job as did the company's front door, although that could not be said about the secretary who worked inside.

She was a tall young blonde with a breathtaking bosom. It was early afternoon but she wore enough makeup to have just finished a modeling session for *Vogue* magazine. Light green eyeshadow that matched her eyes. Heavy mascara. Blusher. She had on a transparent, light-colored lipstick. She stood up when Digger entered to show off her chest and her equally remarkable waist and hips.

She was on the telephone and she motioned with her index finger for Digger to wait. He waited. For her, he would wait until he was eligible for Social Security.

Digger looked at a picture on the wall, a blowup of an old etching of the Graf Zeppelin. When the girl hung up, Digger nodded to the etching. "The pride of your fleet?" he asked.

"Can't beat the gas mileage. Can I help you?"

"If you couldn't, I'm beyond help."

She smiled, a warmer smile than he expected from someone lovely enough to have heard and suffered through every kind of come-on line imaginable.

"Your name is . . . ?" Digger said.

"Me Jane. And you?"

"Lincoln. Elmo Lincoln. I've come to talk to Mr. Baker about insurance on the flight that went down."

She dialed on the intercom. "Mr. Baker, a Mr. Lincoln is here about the insurance."

Before she had even hung up the telephone, the door behind her desk opened and a slight man with thinning dark hair and a pencil-line mustache stepped out. He came toward Digger with the forward momentum of a man about to throw a punch and wanting to get everything he could behind it. The man wore heavy glasses with dark plastic frames; the lenses were tinted blue. Behind them, Digger noticed that Baker seemed to have trouble focusing his eyes. He blinked continuously.

"About time," he said. "Your name is . . ."

"Elmo Lincoln."

"Come on in, Mr. Lincoln."

Digger smiled at the young woman as he passed her. The inside office needed painting as much as the outside of the building did. There were water stains on the walls, and cancerous blotches where chunks of paint had peeled off. Baker almost shoved Digger into a seat in front of the desk, then walked around and sat behind it. He stared at Digger, his eyes flicking nervously.

"Well?" he said.

"Well what?"

"When do we get some money?"

"How much do you want?" Digger said. The office smelled of disinfectant. Or Timothy Baker did. One or the other.

"Now, Lincoln, I don't want you jerking us off. I told the other guy that the replacement value of that plane is four million dollars."

50

"Sounds reasonable to me."

"I don't think you can get away with that shit; that's the book value of the plane. Sure, maybe it was old, but you find me one to replace it. You can't. Four million dollars."

"You got my backing," Digger said. "You going to spend it all on a new plane?"

Baker blinked again. And again. "Maybe and maybe not. It depends on the market. I want to tell you . . . what's your name . . . Lincoln . . . that your attitude is the first reasonable one I've run into since the tragedy."

"How do you think it happened?"

"Well, low-ranking people are always trying to make a name for themselves. A top man like you, he can do what's fair."

"I don't mean my attitude. I mean the accident. How do you think it happened?" Digger said.

"I don't know."

"Was Donnelly a good pilot?"

Baker was drumming the fingers of both hands on his desk. When Digger asked the question, he began to drum faster.

"Donnelly was the best," he said. "He used to be a top captain at Pan-Am. He could fly anything."

"When he was sober," Digger said.

"He was always sober."

"Maybe now, but not always," Digger said.

"Oh, I know that he had a drinking problem years ago. Let's face it, I don't exactly get Charles Lindbergh and Chuck Yeager in here looking for work. But Steve had straightened himself out. Even when he was drinking, he never flew with booze in him. He was always a good pilot."

"You think there was something wrong mechanically? How about a bomb?" Digger looked around the office and thought a bomb might be just what it needed to make it perfect. Cardboard lined one wall and in a corner there was a four-foot-high stack of *Wall Street Journal*s. "The F.A.A. was in here and asking around. Maybe someday if they ever find any wreckage, they can tell what happened, but right now it's all a mystery."

"Everything just went on schedule, the way it was supposed to? Nothing unusual?"

"No, except for the co-pilot and stewardess. Why are you asking so many questions? You know, you've got to pay no matter what was the cause."

"What about the co-pilot and stewardess?"

"Well, he shouldn't have taken off without them. You know this doesn't have anything to do with our claim." Drum, drum, drum, drum, drum. His fingers on the desk were going at four hundred beats a minute. His fingers could serve as transplant material for hummingbirds' hearts, Digger thought.

"I know," Digger said soothingly. "Tell me about the co-pilot and stew."

"I told your other guys. After the co-pilot got sick, the stewardess went off with him to the crew lounge. And while they were gone, Donnelly took off and nobody does that, I mean, we've got regulations and he shouldn't have done that."

"They around?"

"The co-pilot and stew? No. They're on a run up around the northeast. They'll be back tomorrow."

"What are their names?"

"Your other guy has all that in his file."

"Save me looking through paperwork," Digger said. He tried to look friendly and pleasant.

"Randy Batchelor and Melanie Fox. When do you think your company will move?" Baker asked.

"Mine's moving now. Yours, I don't know."

"What does that mean?"

"We don't have the insurance on your plane," Digger said.

"What? Then who . . . what the hell are you doing here? Who are you?"

Digger handed forward a card from his company that did not carry his name. Baker snatched the card from his hand and squinted at it, his eyes blinking, like a high-speed still camera.

His fingers stopped drumming on the desk as if he needed all his energy to focus his eyes.

"Brokers' Surety Life Insurance. What the fuck is that?"

"My company. Right or wrong, but my company."

"What are you here for?" Baker asked.

"Some of the people on the plane had life insurance with us. We're just looking into it."

"What the hell do you want with me? What have I got to do with your goddam life insurance?" He was drumming again with the fingers.

"Nothing. I'm just trying to figure out how the accident happened."

Baker's eyes narrowed. "Wait a minute . . . you people, you're not thinking of trying to make us some kind of party to the claims against you, are you? Jesus Christ, Lincoln."

Digger shook his head. "That's not my decision but I haven't heard it mentioned."

"I'm just trying to get this airline established, for Christ's sake."

"And a good job you're doing, too," Digger said as he walked toward the door. He stopped and said, "Listen, we don't have anything to do with your plane insurance but you know insurance people. They're thicker than thieves so maybe my home office can do you some good."

"Can you do that?"

"I'll try. I honestly will." When Digger left Baker's office the blonde looked at him hopefully as he stepped back into her office. When the door closed, she said, "Everything go all right?"

"I'm going to try to help. What's your name anyway? I can't keep thinking of you as Beautiful Blonde Me Jane."

"Jane Block."

He leaned on her desk. "You been working here long?"

"Seven, eight months . . . jobs are hard to find."

"Not for you," Digger said and meant it. The young woman could have stepped out of the center-fold pages of a man's magazine. "I heard so many stories about this town being Retirement Village, then the first person I meet looks like you."

"Aren't you nice? There's a few of us around."

"Where do the few of you hang out?"

"Here and there." There was no question about it, Digger thought. Coquettishness belonged to youth only.

"Mind if I tag along some night?" he said.

"No, not at all. Tourism is our most important product. The Chamber of Commerce'd be on me if I didn't cooperate."

"Lucky Chamber of Commerce. I'll remind you about that some time. Mr. Baker was telling me about poor Steve Donnelly. Tough accident. Did you know Steve well?"

"Kind of. He was a . . . nice man."

"Not your style?" Digger said.

"A little too churchy-preachy for my taste. But a nice man."

"Can I reach you here?" Digger asked.

"Yes. I'm in the book, too. My home number. Where are you staying?"

Digger thought of Koko and said, "I haven't

gotten moved in yet. Suppose I call you when I'm settled?"

Back at the motel, there were still no messages in his box. Koko was not in the room and there was no note.

Chapter Eight

DIGGER'S LOG:
Tape recording number two, 6 P.M., Tuesday, Julian Burroughs in the matter of Interworld Airways.

Where the hell is Koko?

I bring her and her seven bikinis to beautiful Fort Lauderdale and plop her down in the lap of luxury and she's not even around to untie my shoes after my busy day. What the hell happened to gratitude in this world?

Maybe I'm just too old for her. The generational divide. How old is she anyway? I keep forgetting. I think she's twenty-six. The last birthday I forgot, I think was twenty-six. That's a dozen years younger than me. I don't know if I can deal with somebody that young and that inconsiderate.

To hell with it. Post time.

I didn't tape the sermon by Damien Wardell yesterday morning. I wish I had; he's good. His wife sings all right, too, but she moves funny. I'd like to hear Mother Candace let loose once and sing right. The Reverend Wardell's taste in blondes is not bad, even though I don't do blondes myself.

In the master file are two tapes. First we have an interview with Mrs. Trini Donnelly, wife of our late-lamented skipper. That home could not exactly have been Captain's Paradise for Donnelly. He was a retired drunk turned religious zealot. Trini is a drunk but unretired. The two kids, Spazz and Tard, are typical examples of how, given latter twentieth-century American environment, bad kids can go worse. They know a little too much about fornication for me to believe that Trini has been any rival to Ulysses' wife in the fidelity department. She seems, though, to keep faithful track of money.

I don't think she's got any reason to sue. If her husband wants to leave money to Reverend Wardell, that's his business.

She was a stewardess. She's got to be forty now, her oldest kid is maybe nine or ten. Make her married at thirty. I think all stewardesses get married by thirty. California's contribution to American life: another Great Divide. Thirty is it and if a woman hasn't done it by then, she's not going to do it. Toss her out and try again with two fifteen-year-olds.

Trini says that Donnelly was a top pilot. So does everybody. Probably he was. Then what happened to the plane? Maybe somebody packed him a linguini lunch with an exploding clam in it. Do wives kill for fifty thousand? Mine would. The real desperate ones would.

Donnelly had a lot of drinking and gambling debts to pay off, and Trini was suspicious of Mrs. Wardell and her husband. What is all that about? I've got to ask Kwash to find out if the F.A.A. discovered anything. Although what the F.A.A. can know without wreckage or bodies is beyond me.

Next is a recording with Lieutenant Michael Mannion, who doesn't like me because he thinks I'm part of the giant international fender conspiracy, but that's all right. Detective Dave Coley might help if the price is right. I think I'm going to have him run the passenger list through the police files and see if anybody comes up a Mad Bomber.

Second tape is Timothy Baker, president and chief executive officer and coffee maker at Interworld Airways. His sense of loss is restricted to one of his planes going down and when does he get his insurance money. He wants four million for the tub he lost and maybe that *is* its replacement value. How much could you get nowadays for Lindbergh's *Spirit of St. Louis?* I think a four-million-dollar transfusion might be just what the doctor ordered up for Interworld.

Baker said that the co-pilot and the stewardess missed the flight. Donnelly took off without them. That's got to mean something.

Question: Is a plane crash the best thing that ever happened to Timothy Baker?

Answer: Take Jane Block to dinner and find out. She's in the book.

Where the hell is Koko? I don't really like blondes and shouldn't be driven into consorting with them. I'm too blond myself to trust another one. Let's face it, Koko is short. She's a full foot shorter than me, but she's smarter than me. She says that's not much because everybody is.

Koko is always ragging me that I should have stayed with my ex-wife. I should have kept managing that small loan company instead of moving to Las Vegas and becoming a degenerate gambler. I should have stayed with my kids, What's-his-name and the girl.

I think that's why I like Koko. When she wants to talk to me, she talks to me. My first wife used to want to talk about talking. "We've got to talk," she would say and I would say, "We are talking," and she'd say, "No, really talk." And then she'd talk for twenty minutes about talking. By the time she got around to what she really wanted to say, her time was already up.

I hate that. I just want to talk and be talked to. I don't like to have plans for talking laid out as if talking were some kind of cathedral to build or mountain to climb. You just open your mouth and let words come out and that's talking. Koko understands that. She just talks.

If love were possible, I'd love her.

Just for that.

Where the hell is she?

None of these tapes would be complete without the best and most creative part of the day. Recapitulation of expenses. Don't get upset, Kwash. I'm spending for two days and I'm spending for two.

Yesterday: two phone calls to Las Vegas, fourteen dollars. Parking at the airport to pick up Koko, five dollars. Tips to skycaps, five dollars. Somebody had to carry all her bikinis and I've got a bad back. Took her to dinner at this fancy French diner, thirty-nine dollars with tip. Total, sixty-three dollars. Room and rental car by credit card.

Today: phone call to my room, forty cents 'cause I hung on a long time letting it ring; lunch, nine dollars; phone call to Interworld Airways, ten cents; supplies for my room, eleven dollars, Finlandia's not cheap; total, twenty fifty, hell, I'll pick up the fifty cents myself.

Car, room by credit card.

Two-day total, eighty-three dollars.

And so to drink.

Chapter Nine

"Where have you been? It's almost eight o'clock."

"I'm not allowed out until eight?" Koko asked.

"You didn't leave me a note."

"You never read notes. If I left one at the desk, you'd forget to pick it up. If I left one in here, it'd stay unread forever. You'd use it to empty your ashtray into. Get off my case."

"*Your* notes I read. I always read your notes. I look for them and anticipate them with great pleasure."

"This no-frills motel of yours cut out paper and pen first thing. This place is so fucking cheap that the Gideons didn't even leave a Bible in the drawer. If they had, I could have left you a message by underlining key words. In lipstick. There isn't any pen, remember."

"All right. Where were you? Did you find the beach? You don't look tan. You still look yellow."

"I didn't go to the beach," she said. "I was helping you. After you left this morning, a messenger came with a list from Brackler of all the plane victims and addresses and Xeroxes of their insurance applications and so I thought I'd go and check some of them out."

"I knew you couldn't help meddling. So what'd you find out?" Digger asked.

"Nothing. I checked the first four names on the list."

"You had to find out something. Remember Edison?"

"Yeah, I know. Now I know nine hundred things that don't work. I know all about that. I didn't find out anything. Even Edison couldn't find out anything about these four guys. It was easier to invent the light bulb."

"How'd you get around?"

"I took cabs. Sometimes I walked. Do you want to know what little I've got or do you want to ask irrelevant questions?"

"Yes, I want to know, but we have to do this right. Let me set up the tape recorder. And when I ask you how much you spent on cabs, double the amount."

Digger put a fresh tape in the recorder. Meanwhile, Koko took off her flowered blouse and pink skirt. From a dresser drawer she took a pair of shorts and T-shirt and went into the bathroom. Digger watched her walk away. She had wonderful legs, strong and straight. He wondered how a woman could be both long-waisted and long-legged at the same time, but Koko seemed to pull it off.

"When you come out, bring the vodka," he called. "It's in the toilet."

"What's it doing in the toilet?"

"Actually it's in the back of the toilet in the water tank. This place doesn't have ice cubes, either, so I keep it cold that way."

She came out a few minutes later, holding the vodka. She was wearing white shorts and a white T-shirt with a long printed legend. It had a picture of Uncle Sam, looking ferocious, recruiting poster style, pointing an index finger at the looker. Underneath it was printed:

JOIN THE ARMY.
TRAVEL TO FARAWAY,
EXOTIC LANDS. MEET
INTERESTING, EXCITING
PEOPLE,
AND KILL THEM.

She *was* twenty-six. Digger remembered now because he had forgotten her birthday and a week later bought her the T-shirt for a birthday present. It was one of the few gifts he gave her that she had really liked. Mostly he remembered special occasions with bottles of liquor, always vodka, which she accepted gracefully and then reminded him that she didn't drink.

She splashed vodka into Digger's authentic plastic motel glass, recapped the bottle, and returned it to the bathroom. The bottle was only half full, Digger noticed. He probably hadn't put the cap on tight enough and some of it had leaked out. Or evaporated.

Koko returned and sat in the chair. A gold-colored frog that he used as a tie clip was attached to his portable tape recorder by a wire.

"Talk right into the frog," he said, "I don't have any extra mikes."

"Master tape, number three," he announced. "Julian Burroughs in the matter of Interworld Airways, interviewing Miss Tamiko Fanucci, resident of Las Vegas, regarding background checks of air crash victims. Now Miss Fanucci . . ."

"You can call me Koko. Back at the home office, they know we sleep together."

Digger clicked off the tape recorder and rewound it to the beginning. "Koko, we've got to be all business here. You never know what these tapes might be used for."

"C'mon, Digger. You always erase the tapes when you're done with a case. I've seen you. Nobody ever hears these things but you."

"You never know," he said darkly. He pressed the record button. "Master tape, number three. Julian Burroughs in the matter of Interworld Airways, interviewing Miss Tamiko Fanucci regarding background of air crash victims."

"Las Vegas," she said.

"What?"

"You forgot to say I was a resident of Las Vegas. You did that on the other recording."

Digger sighed. "Skip it," he said. "Now, Miss Fanucci, would you tell me where you went when you left your room today?"

"*Our* room. I never would have rented a dirt-bomb like this place. I left here and took a cab to 415 Jesper Street, address of . . . let me look at my notes."

The tape continued to run as she went to her purse and fished out a small spiral-bound notebook and a pen.

"Where'd you get the pen?" Digger asked.

"I bought it."

"Be sure to keep track of it," Digger said.

"The notebook, too," she said. "I went to check on the last known address of Walter Smith. Four-fifteen Jesper Street is a dump. It must have been designed by the same architect who designed this motel. There's a candy store downstairs and four little apartments upstairs. The candy-store owner, Joseph DeRosa, owns the building and rents the apartments. I had a long talk with him. Walter Smith

63

had lived upstairs in the smallest apartment for about nine months. He was a drunk . . . and was in his sixties. He was collecting some kind of Army disability pension. He drank in his room and sometimes, if the weather was good, he'd come down and sit on the stoop and drink wine out of a bottle."

"He lived alone, Miss Fanucci?"

"Right. No relatives that DeRosa knew of. No mail except his check every month. DeRosa didn't know where he came from but he thought Smith had mentioned New York City once."

"That'll be easy to trace," Digger said. "Walter Smith from New York City. We can ask his brother John about him."

"He had no belongings."

"Everybody's got belongings," Digger said. "It's part of belonging."

"Not anymore. He *had* some belongings. He had two pairs of pants and two shirts. He had some underwear and socks. He didn't have a picture or a note or a letter or a newspaper clipping. He had a couple of back copies of *Sports Illustrated.*"

"What happened to that treasure trove?"

"DeRosa kept it for ten days and when no one came, he put it in the garbage. The apartment's already been re-rented. I talked to the new tenant. She's a whore. She said she didn't find anything there that belonged to Walter Smith."

"You believed her?"

"Yes. While I was walking back down the stairs, I heard her moving furniture around. She thought because I was there, he must have had something that she hadn't found yet, but, by God, she was going to as soon as I left."

"Did you get her name, Miss Fanucci?"

"Yeah. Why? You horny?"

"Unbearably."

"Good. I got her name and phone number. Rhonda Horne."

"Rhonda Horne?"

"Yeah. It's a joke, like a stage name. Round-the-horn, get it? Very heavy sexual connotations. I complimented her on it. Hookers love it when you tell them they have great names."

"What else, Miss Fanucci?"

"For God's sakes, stop calling me Miss Fanucci. Then I went to check out Charlie McGovern."

"Address please."

"Ninety-three Leeson Avenue. It was walking distance. It's a flophouse. McGovern stayed there occasionally. A buck-fifty a night, share a barracks and a toilet. One old guy, let's see, Melvin Langsden, knew McGovern and said he used to work at the supermarket carrying bags once in a while but he didn't know anything about him except that he was a boozer. He didn't know where he came from, either. Charlie was around a couple of years, in and out. Nobody knew anything about him."

"That's not unusual in flophouses, Miss Fanucci. Did he have anything to do with Reverend Wardell, did your friend Melvin know?"

"Oh, yeah. Wardell. Just a minute." She turned back her notebook pages. "On Walter Smith, DeRosa told me he used to go to Wardell's church regular, once a week, and for a day after, he'd sober up but then he'd be drinking again." She turned the pages again. "Melvin told me about McGovern, let's see, he said, 'he goes to church a lot but it don't seem to do him much good, 'cause he ain't never got no money and he still sleeps here. Where is he anyway?' See, he didn't know Charlie was dead. I told him."

"How'd he take it?"

"Hard. He asked me to buy him a drink."

"Did you?"

"I gave him two bucks."

"Be sure to put it on your expenses, Miss Fanucci."

"Oh, I will, Mister Burroughs. Yes, sir, Mister Burroughs. I'm going to put it right down there, that two bucks, and if Mister Brackler comes to town, I'm going to play up to him and see if I can get it up to four dollars, *Mister* Burroughs."

"Goddamit, now I'm going to have to erase that part of the tape."

"Leave it on, erase it later if you want. So from Charlie McGovern's flophouse, I took a cab, I've got a note on it here, three-fifty including tip, and I went to check out James Ernlist. He existed, but just barely. He was a waiter at the Silver Spoon Restaurant. No family, he lived alone in a furnished room in a private house. His landlady, a Mrs. Sylvie Portloy, said that he was nice and quiet and didn't bring anybody home to his room. She said he talked about Reverend Wardell like he was some kind of god or something. He lived there about a year. She kept his personal effects and let me look through them. She thought it was kind of thrilling that somebody from her house was killed in an accident. There wasn't anything in his stuff. A couple of yellow newspaper clippings about Fred Ernlist setting touchdown records at Union Hill High School. That's in Union City, New Jersey. The clippings looked like they were twenty years old. There was a clipping about Fred dying in Vietnam. It said he was survived by his father, James, predeceased by his mother, Mildred. No mention of brothers or sisters. So the way I figure it, that was his kid who died and maybe he went to the bottle because he didn't have a family and he wound up down here."

"Probably," Digger said. "That sounds right. If you're going to be miserable anyway, you might as well be warm."

"I double checked at the Silver Spoon Restaurant. He had worked there about three years. The manager, a Dominick Attas, said that Ernlist was a drifter. He was a good waiter but he missed more than his share of days, out sick. He had a drinking problem, Attas said. He never talked about his family and he didn't have any friends or girlfriend or anything. He had a cable television hookup in his room. He watched sports like twenty-four hours a day. They've got some kind of sports network. . . ."

"I know," Digger said. "You can use it to watch last week's car races. It's as exciting as watching water evaporate. Did you cab it to the Silver Spoon?"

"No, I walked again. It was only a couple of blocks from Ernlist's room."

"And where from there?"

"The fourth name on your list was Anthony Montivini. His address doesn't exist. It's an empty lot."

"Maybe the building was just torn down."

"No, I checked. It was always an empty lot."

"Well, you've already earned your salary," Digger said. "I don't think the company has to pay if the guy put down a spook address."

"You mean I already saved your company a hundred and fifty thousand dollars?"

"It looks that way."

"Shit, Digger, this work's easy."

"Don't let on. I've got Brackler conned."

"Well, I know what we're going to do. We're

going to take some of that saved company money and you're going to buy me dinner tonight at a place with real paper napkins and genuine stainless steel forks."

"Should we do that before or after making love?"

"Instead of," Koko said coldly. "I haven't forgotten how you tricked me into coming down here."

Chapter Ten

Added to the master file is an interview conducted by me at approximately 8:30 P.M. tonight with Miss Tamiko Fanucci, resident of Las Vegas.

Miss Fanucci, on temporary duty for old Benevolent and Saintly, attempted to find the background data on four of the persons believed to have died in the Interworld crash. Those four are Walter Smith, Charles McGovern, James Ernlist, and Anthony Montivini.

The Montivini address given on the insurance application is nonexistent and Miss Fanucci could find nothing about him. The other three men lived at the addresses they gave. None of them had families. Each was known to have known Reverend Wardell.

I spoke on the telephone tonight with Detective David Coley who will run the passenger list through the police department records to see if there is someone with an interesting police record.

The investigation is continuing. I guess I am going to have to talk to the Reverend Wardell. I want to meet the man who is so universally loved that forty people made him their insurance beneficiary. Just before their plane conveniently vanishes.

Koko is sleeping. We had dinner tonight. She knows how to find expensive restaurants, that's for sure. But she may have saved the company a hundred and fifty thousand dollars today so I'm sure Kwash will approve.

She's keeping her own record of expenses. My expenses tonight: dinner for two, one hundred and seventeen dollars. I'll pick up the dime for the telephone call to Detective Coley.

Koko is wearing all her underwear. Jane Block gets more and more interesting. Even if I don't like blondes.

I wish I knew why that plane went down.

Chapter Eleven

Koko had already left the room when Digger dialed Interworld Airways.

"Hello, me-Jane, this is me-Elmo. I was wondering if you were free for lunch. Failing that, are you reasonable for lunch?"

"I would have been more reasonable for dinner last night, but okay."

They met at a small pseudo-French café just off the strip of million-dollar-a-millimeter ocean frontage that made up Fort Lauderdale's famous Galt Ocean Mile. Jane was wearing a red-and-white-striped pullover shirt and short white shorts and white high heels.

"Kind of casual wear for the office, isn't it?" Digger said.

"You know our office. It's not exactly overrun by tourists, but I keep a wraparound skirt in the closet in case I have to look decent in a hurry."

"You'll never have that problem with me. Indecent will do just fine." Digger ordered a vodka for himself and looked at her.

"I don't drink," she said. "Just a Perrier."

"I knew there was something that kept you from being perfect," he said.

When the drinks came Jane asked for a menu. Digger passed.

"Aren't you eating?"

"I'm drinking."

"You can't do both?"

"Not if I want to concentrate on my drinking. Go ahead, don't let me inhibit you."

While she studied the menu, Digger studied her. The young woman was breathtakingly beautiful. The thought of her buried away from the world in a quonset hut at the end of the Fort Lauderdale airport was as big an obscenity as thinking of diamonds never mined, laying for all eternity under twenty feet of dirt and stone.

When the waiter came back, Digger said, "She'll have the rabbit food."

"Beg pardon?"

"The chef's salad. With roquefort dressing. Moldy cheese made into goo is just what rabbit food needs to make it a perfect meal."

"Very good. And you, sir?"

"Another vodka."

"Will that be all?"

"No. Make it a double."

"What kind of a name is Elmo?" Jane asked.

"My father wanted a girl. He wanted to name her after my rich aunt, Aunt Alma. I guess he figured that was the way to get her money when she died. Then, instead of getting a girl, he got me. Well, he couldn't call me Alma. Well, maybe he could if he was Johnny Cash. I mean, you can name a boy Sue. But Alma? But he thought if he named me Elmo, he might be able to get over on my aunt, impress her with the depth of his devotion."

"Did it work?"

"Not a chance. She died and left all her money to my uncle, my father's brother. He had two daughters. He named them Mary and Margaret."

"That's a stupid story. It doesn't make any sense."

"I've got a stupid family. Aunt Alma was the stupidest of all. But she was rich. She used to buy day-old bread. She had a closet full of it. I'd go to visit her and she'd feed me bread. A lot of times it had green mold on it and she'd tell me to eat it because it was penicillin and it'd stop me from getting gonorrhea. I didn't even know what gonorrhea was. I was seven years old."

"Did you eat the bread?"

"I ate around the mold. I fed the mold to her pet parrot. The parrot died before Aunt Alma. I think he had gonorrhea."

"I think you're crazy," Jane said.

"No. Aunt Alma was crazy. Well, maybe I am crazy, a little crazy. My boss thinks I'm crazy."

"Why?"

"He thinks everybody's crazy. That's Walter Brackler, but I call him Kwash 'cause he looks like he has kwashiorkor, a body-shriveling disease. He likes being in the insurance business. That tells you how sane *he* is."

"How'd you get into the insurance business?"

"I'll show you my scars if you show me yours. How'd you get to work for Timothy Baker and Crash Airways?"

"Don't make fun of the folks who pay the rent. I was in college in Boston. I'm from Lauderdale."

"Boston's nice. If you get bored, you can go downtown and watch birds fly into buildings."

"And that's about all you can do. Half the city is townies and the other half is gownies. All the college kids, the males anyway, are gay. The girls all have three names and no brains. So much for one's college compatriots. And then, the townies. The Irish hate the Italians. Both of them hate the blacks. The blacks hate everybody. All of them hate anybody from out of town. Some cities, some sections, you can't drive through at night. Most of Boston, you can't drive through in the daytime. I left after a year and came back to Lauderdale and no big deal, I answered an ad in the paper for a Girl Friday. Christ, I hate that title. Mr. Baker hired me. He was just starting the airline."

"You didn't invest in it, did you?"

"Why, you trying to unload some swamp land?"

"No, do I look like the type? No, it's just that Baker looks a little underfinanced to me and I was wondering how he gets the money to start an airline."

"He used to be in some kind of big management job in New York. He got some investors together. They bought up an old Florida airline and changed the name and bought some used planes. But business hasn't been very good. I think his investors are breathing down his neck."

"They do that when they don't get any return on their money. When'd that all happen?"

"Almost three years. I've been here since the start."

"And now, you're going to be in on the finish?"

"What do you mean?"

"A missing plane, presumed crashed, isn't going to flood your airline with business, is it?"

"No. And, of course, it's a tragedy, but I . . . I don't know. . . ."

"You don't know what?"

"If the insurance company pays off, I think Mr. Baker would buy some good equipment. Better planes. Somehow I think . . . you know, I don't know anything, but somehow I think . . . I've heard him talking sometimes and I think some more money into the company could help us turn the corner."

"There's a good side to everything?" Digger said.

"You make it sound heartless. I don't mean it like that."

"I know, but has Mr. Baker ever talked about buying another plane?"

"Only all the time. Will you be able to help him get his insurance, Elmo?"

"I'm going to try. But I've got my own job to do, too."

"I never did figure out what your job is."

"Didn't Mr. Baker tell you?"

"Only that you had something to do with life insurance on the passengers?"

Digger nodded. "The pilot too. Just checking out claims, all detail work. I've got to talk to the co-pilot and the stewardess and then I'll about have a wrap on this."

"They weren't even on the flight."

"I know, but you know how insurance companies are. Paper work. Talk, talk, talk. Write, write, write. When the pile of paper costs more than the claim, pay the claim. What was that co-pilot's name?"

"Randy Batchelor."

"Is that a name or a title?"

She giggled. "Both, I guess. He just got back this morning. Melanie, too."

"That's the stew," Digger said.

"Ah, yes. Melanie Fox. The Queen of the Skies. One of our stewardi. Or flight attendants, as she'll be sure to tell you."

"How do I reach them?" Digger asked.

She paused, a forkful of salad hovering near her mouth. "I don't know," she said. "I don't think . . ."

"Listen, Jane, I'll tell you something I didn't even tell Baker. Steve Donnelly filled out some kind of insurance form with us, but there's a mix-up on the beneficiary. His wife and his kids have a chance of not winding up with a dime. I'm trying to straighten that out. Maybe Randy and Melanie can help."

She chewed slowly as she thought.

"Well, call me at the office and I'll give you their addresses."

"One other thing and it's really important," Digger said. "Steve's medical record."

"Oh, I couldn't do that," she said.

"Just take a peek at it and let me know what's in it. Maybe there's some kind of insurance examination from some time back. It might help his wife. And those poor sweet little boys."

"All right, I'll try. Call me when I get back to the office."

"Sure," he said. "You're doing a good thing and I'm going to try to help. Mrs. Donnelly. *And* Interworld."

"Maybe we could talk about it over dinner tonight?"

"I don't know. I'll try but I don't think I'll be able to swing it."

"Why not?"

"I've got somebody from the home office with me."

"Bring him, we'll ditch him later."

"It's a her. Some old grouchy harridan dastard. That's it, a dastard. She's got the room next to me and she listens at the wall. She's on the phone with my office twelve times a day."

"Poison her," Jane suggested.

"I can't. I think she's immune. I think she's a secret drinker and she's getting jaundice 'cause she's this funny color, like yellow. All that alcohol and she can't catch anything."

"Try to ditch her."

"I'll try." He looked at her beautiful bosom, as

had every other man in the restaurant, and said it again. "I'll try."

Randy Batchelor's apartment was in a long, low, three-story building in the shape of a backward C. There was parking for tenants on both sides of the building and, without looking, Digger knew there would be a pool in back, inside the arms of the C, with a large ice machine, chaise lounges, patio tables, and a lot of young women.

As he drove into the parking lot, a young man with dark hair and a Clark Gable mustache walked from the side exit of the building. He was wearing white trousers, a blue Navy blazer and a yachtsman's cap. The cap was bent down on both sides, toward the ears, in the style that World War II pilots used to affect. It was called a fifty-mission crush, implying that its wearer had flown so many missions that the earphones he wore over his hat had permanently crushed it into that peculiar saddle-shape.

The young man strolled toward a brown Porsche and Digger glanced at the license plates. There were no numbers; just the word FLYBOY.

He walked to the car just as the young man was unlocking the door.

The man turned around, startled, to look up at Digger, who at six-feet-three was four or five inches taller than he was.

"Yes?"

There was a hint of nervousness in the voice and Digger jumped on it.

"Glad I caught you here, Batchelor. Might save you a trip downtown."

"Who are you? What's this . . ."

"Name's Lincoln. I'm looking into that plane crash."

"The F.A.A.? I already talked to . . ."

"I'm working with the local police, too. They put me on to you. I need a couple of questions answered." Digger leaned against the fender of the car and lit a cigarette.

"You want to go inside, Officer. . . ."

"Lincoln. No. Here's all right. And nobody calls us officer anymore. Here's fine."

Territoriality, Digger knew, was one of the keys to interviewing. When you wanted people to be at ease, you interviewed them at their homes, in their offices, wherever they felt comfortable. When you wanted them to be a little on edge, you tried to talk to them in uncomfortable places where their discomfort level worked for you. Digger had found what he considered the best middle ground: he interviewed people in bars, whenever he could, because most people were ill at ease in unfamiliar surroundings and Digger was as comfortable as a clam in silt. But parking lots were okay, too.

"What can I do for you?" Batchelor said. He noisily glanced at his watch.

Digger pressed. "If you've got an appointment or something, we can arrange something later. Downtown."

"No, no, that's all right. What is it you want?"

"Just tell me how it was you weren't on that death flight?"

"Death flight? Christ, you sound like the *National Enquirer*. I already told your people."

"Yes, and there's a report drifting somewhere through channels and it'll be on my desk in a month or a year, but in the meantime, it'd help if you told me yourself."

"Okay. I went into the cockpit where Steve was. I got sick. Upchucking goddam pukey throwuppy sick. I went back to the crew lounge. I couldn't even walk. Foxy had to help me."

"Foxy?" Digger made a show of writing down the name.

"Our stew. Melanie Fox. It's a nickname, for Christ's sakes. We call her Foxy."

"Oh, I see." Digger made an equally large display of crossing out Foxy from his note pad. Notes were nonsense. He could feel his tape recorder vibrating gently against his back. The open-mouthed frog tie clip that housed the unit's microphone was picking up more of Randy Batchelor than notes ever could.

"Anyway, we were in the lounge and I was heaving like I had morning sickness and before we got back to the plane, Steve is taking off. It's too late to do anything about it, so we're left there holding our hands on our asses."

"Very strange."

Batchelor shrugged. "I guess. I know a lot of times pilots take off without passengers. They leave some of them behind. I almost did that once. I had a charter out of Pittsburgh and I was so goddam busy getting the plane ready that when the tower told me I was cleared to move into takeoff position, I forgot that I was still waiting for these corporate bigshots. So it happens. Stews are left behind a lot, especially if they're a couple of minutes late. But not cockpit crew. That's weird."

"It certainly is. In all my years of experience with planes, I don't think I've ever heard anything like that," Digger said. "What do you think happened?"

"I don't know. The flight was a local. Steve could handle a hundred like that by himself. You wouldn't want a better pilot."

"I understand he had a drinking problem?"

Batchelor shook his head. "No, that's not right.

He had one once but that was a long time ago. He didn't believe in drinking anymore."

"Sounds born again," Digger said casually.

"Something like that. He was in a church and he had straightened out. No more booze. I thought he was nuts because he was a good drinking buddy in the old days but who knows what gets into people. He was so good lately he was a pain in the ass." He glanced at his watch again.

"I'll only be a few more minutes," Digger said. "Whose idea was it that you leave the plane when you got sick?"

Batchelor thought for a moment. Then a look of understanding came over his face. "It was Steve's," he said. He thought some more. "Sure. It was Steve's. I was feeling like cooked shit and he said, better go back to the crew lounge. Get some Pepto-Bismol or something. The walking would do me good. Yeah. That's right. And he told Foxy to go with me to make sure I was all right."

He stopped, looking off into space as if he had just understood something that had been puzzling him for a long while. Digger looked at him carefully, wondering what he had just discovered.

"The passengers were aboard by then?" Digger asked.

"Huh? Oh, yeah. I guess they all were."

"Did you fly with Captain Donnelly a lot?"

"I was here first when Interworld first opened. Then Steve came. We were generally a team. He had stopped drinking but we still used to bounce around a little. Then he got religion and we didn't bounce much . . . I don't know, I always thought religion was supposed to make you happy, but he wasn't exactly Maurice Chevalier."

"Few of us are," Digger said. "It's so hard to

whistle while you're dancing. Were you close friends?"

"Like how?"

"You know. Golf together. Weekends at the old cabin in the woods. Make-believe business trips out of town. Wives and husbands together for a four-hand game of gossip. You know what I mean."

"No, never like that. Steve was too inside himself lately. And I never liked his wife."

There was something in the way Randy answered that last question, Digger thought. Wasn't there? It seemed as though Randy was no longer worried about Digger, but something entirely different.

"When you saw the plane taking off, what did you do?"

"I said 'shit.'"

"Nothing else?"

"What else? Throw rocks at it?"

Batchelor glanced at his watch again. "Listen, I really . . ."

"It's all right," Digger said. "I'm done for now. If anything else comes up, I'll be in touch. Thanks for your time."

Batchelor nodded and turned to the car door.

"One last thing," Digger said. "Any ideas on what caused the accident?"

"Got me. Mind if I go? Some women aren't meant to be kept waiting." He smiled conspiratorially at Digger who winked and nodded.

Digger walked back to his own car. For all his hurry to depart, Digger noticed that Batchelor was taking his time. He had started his engine but he was just sitting behind the wheel, apparently deep in thought. Then he backed the car out of the space and sped away.

Digger watched the FLYBOY license plate turn onto the street. A thirty-five-thousand-dollar car. The fifty-mission crush in a yachting cap, for Christ's sakes.

Batchelor was a little too flashy, for Digger's taste.

Chapter Twelve

Every old city was laid out the same way, Digger thought. There was a poor and busy central core, surrounded by a not-so-poor, not-so-busy ring. Then from the ring came four spokes. One led to the rich section and the opposite spoke led to the poor neighborhoods. The other two spokes led to middling sections. Melanie Fox lived in one of the middling sections.

The stewardess had tired brown eyes, the color of a cooked steak that had been left in the refrigerator too long. They were in a pretty face but the face was tired, too. There were lines at the corners of her eyes and from the corners of her nose to her mouth, and they were mileage marks, not laughter lines. Her body was bounteous, ripe and full, but only one clock-tick away from being a good middle-aged body instead of a wonderful young body.

It was late afternoon and her dark brown hair was messed. She was wearing a long dressing gown when she let Digger into the apartment and he surmised that she had not been out of bed for long.

"Mister Lincoln," she said, looking Digger over as he stepped through the doorway.

"I'm sorry if I woke you when I called. Please call me Elmo."

"Elmo?"

"Elmo."

83

"Come on. Nobody's named Elmo except some guy who eats nails and lifts weights in a circus."

"It's a long story," Digger said. He found himself talking to her back. She was walking across the soft pile carpeting to the sofa with the indifferent ease of a woman who was not terribly frightened by the idea of having a strange man in her home.

"I'll call you Abraham," she said as Digger closed the door. "I'm just having coffee. Want some?"

"I'd rather have a drink but if you're into coffee . . ."

"Have coffee, then a drink," she said. "I don't know if my stomach's up to watching somebody drink this early."

Digger sat in a chair facing the sofa, across the glass-topped coffee table. There were two cups on the table and she poured coffee from an electric pot, connected by a long white extension cord to a wall socket across the room.

She took a long sip of her coffee. "So," she said. It was a question.

"I'm doing a routine check into the accident. International Association for Plane Travel Safety. Eye-APTS. We're an international consortium of private and governmental boards and agencies charged with the responsibility of . . ."

"Spare me the brutal details," she said. "I'm too tired to remember it and too bored to be impressed. What do you want to talk about?"

"I was talking to Mr. Batchelor about the accident."

"I don't know what I can tell you that he didn't. Christ, coffee's good. I don't think I'd want to live in a world without coffee."

"Or women."

"Or men."

"Or vodka."

"You win," she said, laughing. "I'll get you that drink."

"I thought I was going to have to beat it out of you."

"Not me. I'm a piece of cake," she said. She walked into the kitchen, her voice carrying to him from the other room.

"So what do you want to ask me?"

"Do you want me to roar my questions at the top of my voice?" Digger asked.

"No. You can come out here."

In the kitchen, Digger saw she had poured two large glasses of vodka, no mix. She nodded toward the kitchen table. Women love to sit at kitchen tables.

"I'm just wondering if you had any idea about the accident. How it happened."

She shook her head. "It's hard to figure. Steve could've flown that plane in his sleep. So scratch pilot error. What's left? A bomb? A lunatic? Equipment failure? Instrument failure? I don't know."

"Captain Donnelly was good, wasn't he?"

"The best. We were at Pan-Am together and he was a top captain. That was . . ."

"Before he started drinking," Digger said.

She looked at him in surprise.

"I told you. I talked to Batchelor. And I talked to Mrs. Donnelly before that."

"*She* ought to know about his drinking."

"I know she'd drive me to drink," Digger said amiably.

"Anyone. Listen, Abraham. Hey, you don't mind, I just can't call you Elmo, I couldn't call a cocker spaniel Elmo. How deep are you digging into this? Why don't you just get the F.A.A. report when it's done?"

"Look, let's level. I'm not a cop. I'm not some

kind of newspaper snoop or government inspector. All I do is go around and try to figure out how things happened so that just maybe they don't happen again. So I look at everything. People's frame of mind. Equipment. Procedures. Lunatics. You name it, maybe it's important to me. I don't know until I have it all figured out."

She sipped her drink and stared at him. The liquor was startng to erase the washed-out look from her eyes. Finally, she nodded and said, "Go ahead, ask away. I'll tell you anything I know." She said it as if she had weighed all the alternatives and, reluctantly, this was the only possible decision.

"All right. Why don't you like Mrs. Donnelly?"

She hesitated. "I . . ."

"You said anything."

"I guess I did. My big heart gets me into trouble again. Aren't you hot in that jacket?"

"No."

The question made her conscious of her own robe and she pulled it tighter around her shoulders, covering up her deep cleavage. She sipped at her drink, then swallowed it quickly. "Steve and I were lovers when we both worked for Pan-Am. I'm sorry you never met him. There was never anybody quite like him. He was happy and fun-loving and good-natured and I don't think there was anybody in the world who knew him who didn't love him."

"What happened?"

"Trini happened. She came along and made a run at him and she got him all messed up. We all knew what was happening but you can't talk a man out of anything like that. She got him messed up."

"How'd she do that?"

"She got knocked up. So Steve, being Steve, married her. Then he found out she was a bitch on wheels. She wanted, she wanted, she wanted. She slept around. She drank like a goddam camel after three months in the desert. That's when Steve started drinking. I still used to fly with him, but the heart was out of him. He was so damned low all the time. Then I left and I kind of lost touch."

"Why'd you leave?" Digger asked.

"A man. I got married. All very professional. Marriage, fights, separation, and divorce. It would have all fit in one week in a soap opera. I moved back to Atlanta with my folks and I was out of the business for a long time. I used to hear about Steve from friends. Then he left Pan-Am. They told me that the booze was really bad. Finally, I moved down here and found a job with Interworld and who's there but Steve."

"How long ago was that?"

"Two years or so."

"What was he like then?"

"It's funny. He had stopped drinking, so I guess his health was better, but I didn't really see him when he was heavy on the sauce so I don't know. He was still unhappy, though, you could tell."

"No chance of picking up where you left off?"

"No. You're going to laugh at this," she said. "But he got religion. There's this minister in town . . . Reverend Dariell or something."

"Wardell?"

"Yeah. Anyway, Steve was going to this guy and he was different, really different. He was off the juice and he was straight arrow with his wife. He even gave up smoking not too long ago. It wasn't like the old days but at least he seemed happy."

"You think it was this Reverend Wardell?"

"Steve said it was. He always talked about him, tried to get us to go with him to church. That was a laugh. I mean, Randy and I, we're not your average church types, but I don't know, if Wardell could bottle whatever it is he's got, I'd buy some and take it every day."

"Vodka's the closest thing I know in a bottle. Mind if I help myself?"

"No. Do mine, too. The change in Steve was really good to see."

"But it didn't last," Digger said.

"How'd you know that?"

"I don't know. Your tone of voice or something. What happened?"

"A few months ago, suddenly he became like edgy. You know how sometimes a guy's been dry for a while without any problems, and then all of a sudden staying away from the booze really gets to be too much for him."

"Do you think it was the liquor?"

"No. He still wasn't drinking. But he was edgy. He started smoking again. Thanks. Cheers, Abraham."

They clicked glasses.

"What about the night of the flight? How do you explain his taking off without you? You think his mood might have had something to do with that?"

"I've thought about that every day since then and I don't know. I just don't know," she said.

"Maybe something unusual happened that you just don't recall. How about the passengers? What were they like?"

"Stiffs. But it's what you expect when you're flying religious nuts. Actually, though, these were older than most. And usually people come on the plane for a charter and they're partying. These people were, I don't know, quieter, I guess. Some of them, I think, already had a whack on 'cause they were asleep as soon as they hit the seats. That's normal though in charters."

"None of them said anything to you?"

"Nope." She thought about it for a moment, then shook her head and repeated, "Nope."

"What about Batchelor getting sick?"

"He was the last one on the plane. He's always the last one on, even though the co-pilot's supposed to be on first and do the slug work in the flight cabin. Steve never complained about it; he was that kind of guy. So Randy waltzes in late and sits down and he's ready to go to work. Then a couple of minutes later, he got sick and started to throw up. Maybe he drank too much or smoked something or something. If he did, he didn't tell me, but he didn't look it."

"Did he have anything on the plane?"

"No. They're too busy for anything like that. No." She sipped hard at her drink. "He had some coffee. Steve always used to tease me about the plane's coffee, how bad it was, so he always brought a thermos and the first thing he did was pour some out. Randy'd always come in and drink some."

"Why'd you take Batchelor to the lounge?"

"Steve was worried about him. He told me to, in case he needed help. Steve trusted me to make a good decision and let him know, like, if Randy couldn't fly and we'd have to get somebody else. The passengers could get along without me for a while so I went."

"When did you find out Captain Donnelly had taken off?"

"Randy vomited some and then he was okay. We got out of the lounge and went back to the gate but the plane was already gone."

She started to say something else but the question popped into Digger's mind and he cut her off. "What'd you do then? Exactly."

"What was to do? We watched." Digger noticed that she seemed to twist uncomfortably in her chair.

"You might have gone upstairs and told the traffic controllers."

"We didn't think of it," she said, but there was a sharp defensive edge on her voice.

"Melanie, look. I'm not trying to get anybody in the soup. No government agency's going to see my report. I'm really more like working for the airlines. I just want to know what happened. I can't believe that neither of you thought of going up and trying to contact the plane from the tower."

She drank some more of her vodka and Digger got up and brought the bottle and a tray of ice cubes back to the table. He touched her neck as he passed her.

"What did Randy tell you?" she asked.

"Nothing. I forgot to ask him."

"Okay. We had good intentions and we're both probably going to get reamed by the F.A.A. in its report. We were going to go upstairs but Randy said if we did that, Steve'd get into trouble. The flight was a quick and easy one so why not just let it slide? We could hop another plane down to P.R. and fly back with Steve. No one ever had to know. The only squawk might come from a couple of passengers when they didn't get a drink or something, but who'd know otherwise?"

"Makes sense to me," Digger said.

"Us, too. But then the tower, we heard that the tower lost contact with the plane and Steve didn't answer the radio. So we had to go upstairs and report what happened, just to cover ourselves. And you know what happened then. Poor Steve."

"Wife and kids, too."

"Kids anyway," she said bitterly.

"What about Batchelor? How'd he get along with Captain Donnelly?"

"Randy gets along with everybody."

"Donnelly wasn't standing between him and a promotion or something?"

"No, nothing like that. You don't know anything about how airlines work, do you?"

"Not really."

"Honest Abe," she said. "How'd you get a job like this?"

"My uncle is connected."

"Good for you and your uncle. I wish I was connected. Maybe then, my age, I wouldn't be scratching around this place."

"Your age? C'mon."

"Yeah, my age. I'm all right now but it won't be long, I ask them coffee, tea or me and it's gonna be coffee or tea. Your uncle married?"

"As married as you can get. Aunt Brunhilde looks like a Russian field weapon."

"Too bad. How about you?"

Digger reached across the table and touched her hand. "Not me, little girl. I'm not the marrying kind."

"Guess I'll have to keep looking."

"Probably best. You wind up being named Mrs. Elmo Lincoln and you'd die of laughing."

"Buy me dinner?"

"I have to make a phone call first," Digger said.

Digger dialed his motel and asked for his room. There was no answer. He waited for the motel operator to come back on the line but after three minutes, he gave up and dialed again. There were no messages, either. Now where the hell was Koko?

"Who'd you call?"

"I'm in town with my supervisor. A crabby old dastard. I've got to keep her happy."

"No deal on dinner then?"

"She's out, so why not? Who knows what she's doing?"

Chapter Thirteen

Melanie Fox spent dinner trying to be charming and eating as if she were about to enter a Mexican bread-and-water prison the next day.

Digger spent dinner picking at food, drinking more vodka, and three times calling his empty room.

After the vodka course and before the coffee-and-vodka course, he found the business card in his wallet and called Detective Dave Coley at home.

"This is Burroughs. Did you get that list today at the motel?"

"Yeah. I got it. I ran it through our files. It's like a drunk tank list. Half of your people had records for drunkenness or fighting or disorderly, all shit cases. You know, we haven't talked about money."

"I thought a couple of hundred dollars," Digger said.

"Is four a couple?"

"I never could count. Four it is."

"I'll drop the reports at your hotel desk when I go to work in the morning," Coley said.

"I'll leave the money in an envelope with your name on it," Digger said. "There's no crazy terrorist bomb-thrower in that batch of names, huh?"

"Nope. The biggest thing was throwing a brick through a saloon window."

"Shit. Thanks anyway."

"My pleasure," Coley said. "Don't forget the envelope."

Back at the table, Melanie Fox ordered cappuccino with sambuca on the side. When the drink came, three coffee beans were floating in the clear thick sticky liquid.

"Do you know the legend of the coffee beans?" she asked.

"Yeah. It's a lesson for our times. Some guy figured out how to raise the price of a buck-and-a-half drink to two and a half bucks by dropping in one cent's worth of coffee beans."

"You're not much of a romantic."

"That's not true," Digger said. "I never met a coffee bean I didn't love."

"I've had enough drinking. Do you want to go to a party?" she asked him.

"A party without drinking?"

"You'll be able to drink if you want," she said. "It's just that there are alternatives."

"Just a minute," he said.

Digger called Koko again. No answer. He came back to the table. "Sure. Let's go to a party."

The party was in a rundown old mansion at the farthest southern end of Lauderdale. By the time Digger and Melanie arrived, there were fifty cars parked near the house, on the street, in the driveway, upon the grown-over lawn. Every car must have arrived packed with people because the giant old house looked and sounded as if it were bulging with life.

A familiar bittersweet aroma wafted through the yard as they approached the house and Digger said, "I love the smell of freshly-lit grass."

"It's like a junkie's garage sale," Melanie said. "Something for every taste."

"Whose house is it anyway?" Digger asked.

"Damned if I know. Randy invited me."

The air hung thick with marijuana smoke when they stepped inside the front door.

Melanie was greeted by only three people, all women, who looked over her shoulder as they were talking and made Digger feel like a lambchop.

"Foxy, it's nice to see you."

"Foxy, it's nice to see you."

"Foxy, it's nice to see you."

"I love honest displays of warmth," Digger said.

"Make yourself at home," Melanie said. "I'm going to look around."

No one spoke to Digger and when he saw that no one was going to volunteer the information on where the bar was, he asked a young woman with red hair and acne scars.

"The kitchen." She pointed toward the back of the house. "I think. If not the kitchen, the patio."

It was the kitchen. A large table had been set up as a bar. There was Chablis, sangria, tequila, and one bottle of Fleischmann's vodka. Digger poured himself a large glass, then when no one was looking, hid the bottle under the sink. Just in case that was all they had.

Glass in hand, he wandered through the crowds, listening, not saying much. The topic on everyone's lips seemed to be the federal government's fascistic infringement on everyone's human rights as demonstrated by their cracking down on drug shipments from Mexico. To listen to these people talk, Digger decided, one would get the impression that marijuana and cocaine were the two basic staples of the American diet, and that bread and vodka were only artifacts of a bygone age.

He saw Melanie Fox sitting on floor cushions in a

corner with three other women. They were passing a joint back and forth along the line. She looked very happy.

He went back to the kitchen and sneaked himself another drink from the bottle under the sink. The bottle was only half full and he was faced with conflicting worries. If he drank it too fast, he would soon wind up without any. On the other hand, if he poured himself a small drink, someone else might find the bottle and drink it all up before Digger could make a reasonable run at it. He voted for the present over the future and filled his glass to the brim. Live today, let tomorrow take care of itself.

Back outside, he saw a face he recognized.

In a far corner of the room, Randy Batchelor was standing, still wearing his crushed yachting cap and blue blazer, a glass in his hand, an amused smile on his lips. As Digger watched, an Amazonian tall blonde sidled up to Batchelor and talked into his ear at close range for a few moments. Batchelor nodded and reached into his jacket pocket and brought out a shiny brass cylinder, approximately the size and shape of a .38 caliber bullet. The woman took it, kissed his cheek, and walked toward the stairs. Very interesting, Digger thought. Randy Batchelor was dispensing cocaine. As he watched, another young woman approached Batchelor, talked to him, and he pointed her in the direction of the stairs, up which the Amazon had just gone. She too kissed his cheek and walked quickly to the stairs.

Digger found a phone in the kitchen and called his room. While the phone rang, he topped his drink. Koko did not answer.

In the living room, a pretty woman put her hands around his waist. He twisted loose before she felt his tape recorder.

"You wanna?" she said. She seemed to think this was very funny patter because she giggled.

"Do I wanna what?"

"You know."

"Not now," Digger said. "I've taken a vow of purity."

"Lemme know when you decide to break it."

Batchelor passed out three more hits of coke as Digger watched from across the room, but he saw no money changing hands. Maybe the flashy young pilot was just a public benefactor. Sure. And the Palestine Liberation Organization was just a group of fun-loving bedouins.

Later, he stopped thinking about Koko. He found the pretty woman who had wanted to.

"Let's," he said.

"Sure," she said.

And they did, amid a pile of coats in one of the upstairs bedrooms. The woman seemed very grateful.

Back downstairs, he drained the last of the vodka from the bottle under the sink and told himself it was a chintzy party. Out in the main room, he looked for Melanie Fox, but he couldn't find her. Nor could he find Randy Batchelor.

He was on his way into the kitchen to deposit his empty glass in the sink, when as good fortune would have it, he turned and looked at the liquor table and saw another bottle of vodka there.

And who said God is dead, he thought. And poured himself another drink.

Chapter Fourteen

It was after 4 A.M. when Digger got back to his room. He bumped quietly against a wall. He couldn't remember that wall being there. He would have sworn that side of the room opened onto a beautiful oriental garden.

"Excuse me," he told the wall.

"So there you are, you son of a bitch," Koko said.

"Shhhhh, you'll wake me up," he said.

"Where the hell have you been?"

"Looking for you."

"Did you try here?" Koko asked.

"This was my last hope."

Koko turned on the lamp and the light flooded the dark room, stabbing Digger in the eyeballs. When he could see, Koko was pulling the sheet up to her neck. They stared at each other.

"So it's you," he said. "I was wondering who was in our room."

"You're whacked. What the hell time is it, anyway?"

"I think it's four o'clock."

"You're a son of a bitch."

"You're opinionated, obnoxious, and much too short," Digger said.

"Four o'clock," she intoned.

"Time for beddy-bye," Digger said. He struggled out of his clothes which he dumped onto a chair.

When he got down to his shorts, he peeled away the surgical tape that held the microphone wire to his side and unhooked the thin belt that held the tape recorder around his waist.

He crawled into bed before deciding he needed a cigarette to sleep properly. He got up and brought the pack and lighter back to bed, where he sat down. His head reeled a little. All this getting up and down was not good for him.

Sitting down, he lit a cigarette, then, gingerly, slid under the light sheet.

Koko turned off the light and he felt her shift around and turn her back to him.

"Who were you with?" Her voice seemed to echo in the darkened room.

"The stewardess who was supposed to be on the flight. Her and two hundred other people. Before that, everybody and his brother. The co-pilot who didn't go. The girl from the airlines office."

"Did you have to make it with her?" Koko asked.

"Who?"

"The stewardess."

"I didn't make it with her. I don't think I did."

"You did."

"No, Koko. I really didn't. I think."

"I don't understand it, Digger. You're not *that* good looking. How the hell is it that women bust their bloomers every time you walk near them?"

"It's a trick."

"What's the trick?" she asked.

"You really want to go into this now?"

"What's the trick?"

"All right. It's the only way I'll ever get any sleep, I guess," Digger said. "You start out with all women are in love with their fathers, especially the young ones. So maybe I don't look like their fathers, but I'm big enough to at least look the masculine role model. When I meet them, I touch them a lot. Hands, arms, shoulder, backs. The way their fathers used to touch them. It breaks down their physical resistance. Then I call them things like 'little girl.' It makes women melt. It's a thing their fathers might have called them. Sometimes they don't melt, they ooze."

"How freud-ulent of you, you heartless bastard."

"Koko, you asked me. I didn't volunteer. Remember, this is my job. This is what I do, make people talk. That's another thing women ooze over me for. I listen to them. Really listen. Do you know how seldom somebody listens to a woman, particularly a man? They pretend they're listening but they don't. They're just figuring out what motel they can go to and did they bring enough money and should they take one car or two cars and is she going to want to eat dinner first and all the time she's talking and he's saying 'uhuh, yes, oh really,' and he doesn't hear a fucking word. But I listen. I like to hear women talk. Want to go to the beach tomorrow? Did you go today?"

"No. I worked today. Maybe tomorrow. Get some sleep, Digger."

He stubbed out his cigarette and turned to kiss her but her back was resolutely, coldly toward him. She was wearing panties and bra and a long T-shirt. He turned back, unkissed, and closed his eyes. He would pass up his final quiet cigarette of the day.

"Digger?"

"Yes."

"I'm a little on edge. My sister called tonight and she might have to have an operation."

"What for?"

"Women problems."

"You mean there's an operation for suspicion and narrow-mindedness?"

"Go to sleep," she said sourly.

"Okay."

"Digger?"

"What now?"

"I was out today checking that list. There's something really strange going on here."

"Like what?"

"I'll tell you about it in the morning. When you're sober."

"I hate being told things like that."

"You know, your company is a pack of assholes?"

"Only wake me up for something important," he said.

"So are you," she said.

"I said important," he said.

Chapter Fifteen

DIGGER'S LOG:
Tape recording number three, Julian Burroughs in the matter of Interworld Airways, 11 A.M. Thurdsay.

Koko has gone to the store to get us some coffee. She is off the snot from last night, praised be the name of Jesus, but I have to take her to the beach. I hate the beach. Anyway, I don't know if I deserved her wrath last night. I didn't hit that stewardess, I don't think. Maybe I hit somebody else. I'm not sure. I remember being on a bed with somebody next to an itchy tan jacket. So what?

In the master file are three new tapes, interviews with Jane Block and Randy Batchelor and Melanie Fox and Miss Tamiko Fanucci, resident of Las Vegas.

Jane says Timothy Baker is getting a little heat from his investors in Puddlejumper Airlines. Yes, the crash is a tragedy, etcetera, etcetera, but the insurance money might let him buy some better equipment. He talks about that a lot. Maybe he dreams about it and plans for it and schemes for it and blows up his own plane for it? I just wish Baker could focus his eyes. He makes me uncomfortable.

Randy Batchelor. A pilot with a brown Porsche and FLYBOY on his license plates might do anything, particularly when he's a little nervous. When I was talking to him yesterday afternoon, I suddenly had a feeling that this guy would not be above smuggling stuff from the Caribbean back into America.

Then last night I saw him passing out cocaine like lollipops, so maybe. There was no bad blood between him and the dead pilot. At least, he said so and Melanie confirmed it.

He got sick after drinking some of Donnelly's coffee. How convenient that both of them got off the plane and it took off without them. Suppose they knew the plane was going belly-up? Suppose they arranged it because they were bringing stuff into the United States and Holy Roller, God-fearing Steve Donnelly was going to drop a dime on them? Suppose? Anyway, though, I've got to ask Mrs. Donnelly about that coffee of his.

I think Detective Coley should run a check on these people for me. He checked out my whole list of passengers yesterday, and except for assorted drunk arrests, there wasn't anything there. Thank God I remembered to leave him the four hundred dollars when I got in last night. Otherwise, he might have rung my bell this morning. I need my rest.

Melanie is a loser. Ex-lover of the dead pilot. She seemed a little protective of Batchelor but I don't know if that's just normal protectiveness of crew for crew. She and Randy confirmed that Donnelly used to drink but didn't anymore. But she said that he was back recently to being depressed. Show me depression and I'll show you a reason for it. What reason?

Melanie has no love for Mrs. Donnelly, either. Triangle? Kill the man they both love so her rival can't have him?

No, not after all these years. But maybe, just maybe, she's shitting me about Donnelly. Maybe she's hooked up with Batchelor and Donnelly was going to squeal on them about something? Maybe. Crew can easily smuggle a bomb on a plane.

She said the passengers were juiced when they got on the plane. I guess they suddenly realized they were flying Interworld Airways. I mean, I know this airline, I know what it's like. In a real airline, when the pilot announces that he's taking off and the stewardesses should assume the position, I want them to lie on their backs and spread their legs. Interworld . . . I can see it, stewardesses huddling in corners, covering their hands and eyes and ears with their hands. That's the kind of airline this is. I'm afraid to go to their goddam offices. Who would willingly go on one of their planes?

One thing that was puzzling me. Why didn't Randy and Melanie—Jesus, it sounds like an adagio dance team—why didn't they tell the controllers at the airport that Donnelly was flying alone? She said not to get Donnelly into any trouble.

It's logical. And maybe it's true.

The last segment on the tapes is my interview this morning with Miss Fanucci, regarding her activities yesterday in searching out relatives and friends of the accident victims.

She said last night that everybody in my company, me included, was an asshole. This morning she proved it to my satisfaction. Yesterday she went to the airport insurance machine and picked up one of B.S.L.I.'s handy-dandy applications. Part A, Paragraph One, says it covers "Injuries received while the insured, as a passenger and not as a pilot or crew member, is riding in et cetera, et cetera. . . ." Steve Donnelly's insurance was invalid. B.S.L.I. doesn't have to pay anything to anybody on his death because it's specifically not covered. Pilots can't buy those policies. Why didn't Brackler or somebody in his office catch this? Is it up to me to do everything? Anyway, I don't think I'm going to tell anybody about it right now, just in case it can do me some good to have people thinking Donnelly was insured.

I think Frank Stevens should send Koko an engraved citation. Already she's saved the company three hundred thousand dollars—first on that nonexistent address, second on the Donnelly policy. The girl ain't half bad.

She also came up with another interesting item. First of all, she went to six more addresses of the victims and found five more places where men used to live who had no family and no friends, no past, no present, no future. Most of them were drinkers. That's confirmed by Detective Coley's reports. Two of the five used to go watch Reverend Wardell preach, according to neighbors. The others might have.

The sixth address she went to was something else. This was the furnished room of Charles Stermlieb, the one passenger who didn't have insurance. His landlady, Hildie Walters, said that in the morning hours after the crash, there was a burglary at her house, and the burglar ransacked Stermlieb's room. Nothing appeared to be taken.

But Hildie used to do an occasional piece of laundry for Stermlieb and she found in the pocket of his weary old blue jeans, lo and behold, a filled-out insurance application on one of those airport forms. Koko charmed it out of her. The insurance form is filled out in a neat, precise little hand, block printed, and signed in this illegible scrawl by Stermlieb. I have to ask Kwash to look at the other applications we received and find out if there are any similarities in the handwriting.

Very interesting. And what would someone burgle this nondescript's furnished room for?

Koko is worth her weight in sushi. So far, she's

tracked down ten of the forty passengers. She thinks it's significant that ten out of ten were pretty much social castoffs. So do I.

I guess I'll have to go to that frigging beach. I hate the beach. If you just want to lay around, why do it where there are flies? Why not on your own bed in your own eight-dollar-a-night room.

Koko's civil this morning but she's still mad at me. I can tell. She tied my shoelaces together. Too bad. If she could only learn to control her temper, when I haven't done anything at all wrong, she'd be an exceptional woman. Off-the-scale genius, phi beta kappa at 20, mathematical wizard, knows everything, beautiful, sensitive. Yeah. And a part-time hooker.

Maybe we're reaching the end and we're going to have to find new roommates. Well, if this is the end, then let it be the end, fast and sure. No dragging it out.

A busted romance is like a bird with a broken wing. You keep looking at it and you keep hoping it'll get well, but it never does. It just hops around a little and then it dies.

The day's expenses. Lunch, Jane Block, forty dollars, the girl eats hard. Dinner, Melanie Fox, seventy-eight dollars, she eats even harder. Telephone calls, sixty cents. Research services, four hundred dollars. Total, five-eighteen-sixty. Big day but we saved another hundred and fifty thousand by reading the policy. Kwash, doesn't anybody in your office have any brains?

There's Koko at the door. Hop Harrigan signing off.

Chapter Sixteen

The telephone rang just as Koko came into the room and she picked it up as she set down the paper bag with the wet bottom.

Digger watched as she chatted. The young woman had an infinite capacity for being beautiful. Her skin was as smooth as freshly stirred paint and her eyes actually sparkled. She smiled often, her teeth appearing almost pearlescent against the rose lips that needed no lipstick. She was filled with energy and vitality, but not herky-jerk or frantic, and even as she walked around the room, the phone propped between shoulder and ear, she moved with a dancer's grace.

Finally, she said, "That's really good news. Thanks for calling me. I'll talk to you."

She hung up.

"I don't have to go home. That was my sister and she doesn't need that operation."

"Do you know how many times I've been trapped or tricked into a motel room because a woman told me that her sister or her mother or her daughter needed money for an operation? You're refreshing, I'll say that for you."

"Just honest is all." She ripped the bag open and handed Digger a container of coffee. She also handed him a piece of pastry wrapped in waxed paper, then brought her own over and sat across the table from him. He opened the wax paper slowly.

"Those are almonds," he said.

"These days, that's a find when you buy almond Danish."

"I hate almonds. I specifically asked for cheese Danish."

"No, you didn't. You said you wanted Danish. Cheese, if they had it. I heard you. They didn't have it."

"I hate almonds. Now I have to pick all the almonds off the top of this Danish," he said.

"Eat them, Dig," she said.

"You're in a good mood," he said.

"Yeah, I am. I just came to a decision in my life."

"What's that?" he asked.

"That you're never going to change."

"I could have told you that. I'm always going to be kind and witty and handsome and brilliant. Don't you know better than to talk with your mouth full?"

"You're always going to be crass and insensitive and promiscuous and thoughtless and I guess if I want to put up with you, I put up with that."

"You don't want to change me?"

"How long did your ex-wife try?"

"How long did I know her?"

"Exactly," Koko said. "I'm not even going to try."

"Does this mean we're going to go through life irritating each other?" Digger asked.

"Probably. You can't change. I won't change. This is good Danish. Stop picking off those almonds."

"I hate almonds. They're so goddam skinny in those little slivers and they get between your teeth and hide there for weeks and when they finally come out, they're mushy."

"Is there anything else you don't like?"

"Yes. I don't like French designer shirts 'cause they make them for fags with wrists like broomsticks. I've been thinking about that a lot lately. I don't like most jockey shorts 'cause you can't get it out and once it's out, you can't get it back in."

"Getting it back in never seemed to be much of a concern to you," Koko said.

"Quiet. I don't like cocktail lounges that have those glasses with bumps on the bottom because they always drip water on your pants and it looks like you made wee-wee."

"What else?" she asked.

"I don't like double crostics, because I can never understand the rules. I don't like my mother."

"Reasonable. Nobody likes your mother. Not even your father."

"She never tried to feed me almond Danish," Digger said. "I hate almond Danish. What do you think about this case?"

"I don't know what to think. Ten people, every one of them a cipher. How often do you scratch ten people and find ten without some kind of family?" She shook her head. "But somebody burglarized Stermlieb's room." An almond was stuck to the side of her lip. "I don't understand it," she said. She picked off the almond and ate it. "Save me your almonds, I love them. Listen," she paused, "isn't it about time you went after Wardell? Doesn't everything come back to him and the money?" Koko asked.

"I told you. I went to see him preach. I was impressed."

"I don't mean watch him perform. I mean go talk to him."

"Yeah," Digger said. "I guess I've got to do that. But I'm really delicate at this kind of work. I don't just go plowing ahead."

"No? Let's ask that stewardess. She'd probably swear that you're great at plowing ahead."

"Stop that. No, first I like to study the accident, and then I like to hang around the edges for a while and see who's there and then I jump into the middle."

"That's very logical. Do you really do that?"

Digger thought for a moment. "I guess not," he said. "I guess I do whatever amuses me at the moment." He nodded. "You're right. It's time to talk to Wardell."

"Tomorrow," she said. "Later. Not now. Now we're going to the beach."

"I hope they have a stand that sells cheese Danish."

Chapter Seventeen

Back from the beach. Digger had taken a long cold shower to try to take some of the sting out of his back and shoulders and arms and chest and thighs and calves and knees and neck and face. He congratulated himself on having had the good sense to keep his insteps covered all the time. They weren't burned. That meant, when he committed suicide from the pain, he'd be able to die with his shoes on.

He was shaving delicately in the bathroom, when he heard the telephone ring, and Koko's voice say: "Who?"

The she said, "Just a moment."

She cooed, "Oh, Elmo. It's for you."

He came out of the bathroom, a towel wrapped around his waist and saw Koko covering her face with her hand hiding a mock smirk.

"Here, Elmo," she said sweetly.

"Hello."

"Elmo, this is Jane. That your boss?"

"Yeah."

"She sounds like a bitch."

Digger looked at Koko who had collapsed back on the bed, still wearing her bikini, silently mouthing at him "Elmo" and then giggling.

"That she is," Digger said.

"Listen, I'm sorry it took me so long, but I couldn't find Donnelly's records in the file. And then

111

today I looked again, and they were there. Good health, no problems, I can't read all that stuff, but the doctor's letter said okay. He was due for his physical next month. Dr. Richard Josephson, Harborview Avenue, is the doctor."

"Thank you. That helps."

"You ever going to be able to get away from her?"

"I'm trying," Digger said. "Really trying. I'll let you know."

"Okay. I'll be around."

Digger hung up the telephone.

"If you say anything, I'll slug you," he said.

"Elmo? Elmo what?"

"Elmo Lincoln."

Koko started giggling again.

"Elmo Lincoln," she said. "How'd you meet that one? She come swinging in on a vine?"

"Very funny."

"Why'd you pick the name of some movie Tarzan?"

"I asked her what her name was and she said 'Me Jane.' I couldn't say 'me Tarzan,' could I? Elmo Lincoln just came to mind."

"You're beautiful, Digger. Why didn't you tell her your real name?"

"I forgot. She asked me kind of fast."

"You're crazy. Who is she, anyway? You jump her bones, too?"

"Jane something. She works at the airline. No."

"What'd she say about me?"

"She said you sounded like a particularly evil, but lustful, sex-driven, horny, beautiful bitch. She said she bet I was going to service your account right away."

"And you agreed?"

"Yes."

"Tarzan has more brains than that. So did Cheetah, for that matter. You ain't got a chance, sucker."

"How long are you going to punish me? Didn' I take you to the freaking beach?"

"Sure. You're a bag of fun. You slept all day until you turned the color of a peeled tomato. Then you asked people on the beach if they had cheese Danish to sell. Then all you did was bitch about the sun." She smiled. "You want to make love? Good. We'll do it on the floor. You lay on this genuine indoor-outdoor steel wool rug. I'll get on top. Watch me squirm. Your back will love it."

"I never realized until this minute just how evil and sadistic you Oriental-Sicilians are."

"You don't know anything yet. I'm going to take a bath in musk."

"Musk?"

"Yes. Horny mink musk. And then I'm going to bed and I'm going to smell like a French whore in estrus and if you touch me I'm going to stab you in the balls with a stiletto. I'll teach you to mess with me, Elmo. Elmo. Do you really think I'd give it up to somebody named Elmo?"

Digger went into the bathroom to pour himself a drink, and when he came out, he sat in the chair in front of the television set. Koko went into the bathroom to take a bath. When she came out, Digger was sleeping in the chair. She let him stay there.

At 6 A.M., Digger looked up Dr. Josephson's telephone number and dialed. A tape-recorded message told him that office hours began at 10 A.M. and he could leave a message at the signal, but if he really needed emergency service, fast, Grade-A emergency service, the best thing to do was to go to a hospital. Any hospital.

Digger looked at Koko. The sheet had slipped from her body and her bare breasts invited him to come to bed. He thought about it for a moment, then sat on the edge of the bed, looking at her. She slept on her back in what psychologists called the royal sleep mode, the position assumed by someone who feared no enemies or no danger. She was not just beautiful; she was perfect. Her face was a delicate bronze and her hair was not dark brown but black. Her face, so quick to smile, was unlined.

She was everything he had ever wanted in a woman. She was beautiful and smart and funny and warmhearted. She had never been married and she never talked to Digger about marriage. He couldn't tell if she even thought of being married to him.

They had met in a hotel hallway. She had been naked and just a little drunk. She suffered from a common Japanese inability to handle alcohol, but it was like her not to accept life's or genetics' verdict. She had tried to drink. Someone bought her a drink, then tried to take advantage of her, wound up stealing her purse and pushing her naked into the hallway of the hotel. Digger, in a room across the hall, had gotten back her purse and her clothing and he had gotten her not long after.

Digger had left his wife and children and moved to Las Vegas to gamble. He was just getting over the fever. Soon after, with a little pocketful of winnings, he had bought a condominium on the Las Vegas strip. Then he had done a substantial favor for Frank Stevens, the president of B.S.L.I., and had gotten an occasional job as a claims investigator. And had also gotten his nickname of Digger.

Koko was by then a dealer at the Araby Casino and she had moved in with him.

He worked occasionally. So did she. She dealt at the casino, but once in a while, the casino asked her to "entertain" a visiting high roller with a penchant for oriental women.

Digger couldn't bring himself to complain about it. Maybe it was, in a way, his insurance policy. Could a hooker, even a part-time hooker, expect him to say "let's get married?"

But what if she weren't what she was? What would he do then?

He looked at her again.

Some kinds of beauty were beyond words.

He checked himself from reaching out and touching her hand, tossed up childishly on the pillow beside her face. There was the hint of a smile on her lips.

"Tamiko," he said softly. "I'm an alcoholic and am more than a little crazy. I don't much like myself and I don't think I can like anybody else, much less love them. Except maybe my father. But if I ever loved anybody, it'd be you. Maybe . . . someday . . . . ahhh, bullshit. We're going to be too busy forever, laughing at each other's jokes, telling each other stories. Never happen, kid. And ain't it a fucking shame."

Then he got up and went inside to shower and brush his teeth and look at his beet-red body and curse the sun and the woman who exposed him to it.

Koko was still asleep when he came out. He taped his recorder under his shirt, made sure he had several extra cassettes in his light tan jacket pocket, and wrote her a note with the pen he found in her purse.

"Koko. Went out to find me a kind woman who'll give me some. I don't know if I'll ever return. Have a nice day. Digger."

It was obvious to Digger that Dr. Josephson, for all his medical education, had never been exposed in childhood to the Peter Slump and Peter Posture health books. He sat behind his desk like a soft pile of wet laundry.

"Dr. Josephson, my name is Julian Burroughs."

Josephson shook his head. "I'll never understand. You New Yorkers come down here and refuse to believe that this is the real sun. You hang around out there all day boiling like a lobster, and then come running to a doctor. Did you put anything on that burn?"

"I didn't come for my sunburn, Doctor. I'm fully prepared to suffer in silence for the sin of stupidity."

"What's the problem then?"

Digger handed the doctor one of his business cards. "I'm with the Brokers' Surety Life Insurance Company."

Josephson nodded. He was a huge man and after he stopped nodding, his jowls continued to flap up and down in agreement for what seemed to be another full round trip.

Josephson handed the card back.

"What can I do for you?"

"I'm doing some routine checking for my company before we pay off on some insurance involved in that Interworld air crash a couple of weeks ago."

"Whose insurance did you have?"

"A couple of passengers."

"And how can I help?"

"You were Steve Donnelly's private physician?"

"That's right."

"He was due for a company physical soon."

"Is it a year already?"

"Time flies," Digger said. "At least better than Interworld's planes. I want to know the state of Captain Donnelly's health."

"I've told you people, I don't talk about my patients to third parties. Was Steve one of your insured?"

"I don't really know, Doctor, but I doubt it. Do pilots insure themselves on their own flights?"

"No, probably not. I'm afraid I can't help you."

"You said you told 'us people' that. What people?"

"You and that other fellow yesterday."

"Was he an insurance man?"

"Yes. I don't remember his name though."

"What'd he look like?" Digger asked. "My office messes everything up and it'd be like them to have two men on the same job and not tell either of us."

Josephson shrugged. "I don't know. Nice-looking fellow. Had a mustache."

"Dark wavy hair?" Digger asked. "Kind of good looking?"

"Sounds like him," the doctor said. "I told him like I'm telling you. I don't give out information on patients."

"Could I see Captain Donnelly's file?" Digger persisted.

Josephson glanced toward a file cabinet alongside his desk, before he said, "Of course not. I can't do that."

"It would facilitate my paperwork, Doctor. Get people paid a little faster."

"Sorry, but that's not my concern."

"How would you release the records? To Mrs. Donnelly?"

"Why should she want them? No."

"You're the family doctor?" Digger asked.

"Yes. Steve, Trini, the kids, they're all my patients."

"Thank you, Doctor. I appreciate your giving me this time."

Mrs. Donnelly was not home when Digger telephoned and neither was Koko. However, The Church of the Unvarnished Truth announced that the Reverend Wardell would have private consultations beginning at noon.

Digger hung up and had a drink before driving to Wardell's. He had never met a Messenger of God before and he wanted to be fortified.

The Wardell parsonage was an old white frame building directly behind his mission tent. It was separated from the tent by a private parking lot, large enough for a dozen cars. Digger parked and went up the three stairs to the porch and followed the somewhat-Germanic printed instructions on the door to "Ring Bell, Then Enter." Somewhere, he thought, there was a leftover Nazi from World War II, and he had made a career out of writing America's signs. *Keep off Grass. Shut Door Tight. No Noise Allowed. Jawohl, mein führer.*

He found himself, without instructions, in a large room whose walls were lined with sofas and chairs. He had expected to see some evidence that the Damien Wardell Bible-Reading and Tub-Thumping Society had begun to spend its six-million-dollar windfall, but the sofas and chairs gave no evidence of it. They looked as if they had last been used to furnish Noah's Ark. He sat in one of the chairs, felt a loose spring under his butt, and moved to another chair. He lit a cigarette, but when he could not find an ashtray, he went to the door and tossed the cigarette out into the parking lot.

When he went back inside to sit down, he looked at the magazines on the old cocktail table in front of the sofa. You could tell a lot about people by looking at the magazines in their waiting rooms. Doctors favored *Time* magazine, perhaps to impress the point that time was flying by and they would appreciate your handling their bill promptly before it was too late. Dentists went for golf and boating magazines. Presumably this was to give the victim something pleasant to envision doing when the bloodletting and agony were over and the upper plate still didn't fit. The Reverend Wardell leaned to *Mechanix Illustrated* and *Popular Mechanics*. Build your own solar power generator. Heat your swimming pool for three cents a day. Some startling conclusions about the safety of mopeds. The lowly bean: solution to the world's hunger?

It made Digger wonder what kind of world Wardell envisioned after the second coming. He could picture hordes of smiling drones, mopedding their way, in flatulent bliss, between their bean farms and their heated swimming pools with a solar-powered organ huffing "Amazing Grace" for background music.

His musings were pleasantly interrupted by a door opening. He looked up to see a tall blond woman with an angelic face and devilish body standing in the doorway, crooking her finger toward him. She had green eyes, the exact color of mid-season oak leaves, and a thin band of freckles across her nose. She was wearing tight white jeans that molded themselves snugly around her narrow waist and across her smooth full butt, and a loose-fitting light blue shirt that could not hide her opulent bosom.

"Heavenly," Digger said as he stood.

There was no answering smile on her face. "You are early," she said accusatorily. "The reverend's hours don't begin until noon."

"I couldn't wait to be saved," Digger said. "You got to get up early to beat the devil."

She stared at him for a moment, then turned away. "This way, please," she said.

As Digger followed her through the door, he noticed a large blue handkerchief, matching the color of her shirt, tucked into her left rear pocket. She led him into a small office, nodded him toward a chair and sat down behind a small metal desk. On a stand next to her desk was an old Remington manual typewriter.

"Guess you'll be getting a new typewriter soon," he said casually.

"I beg your pardon," she said.

"Typewriter. That one's pretty old. You'll probably replace it soon," he said.

"It works perfectly well," she said. She opened a manila file folder and picked up a magic marker. "You've come to see the reverend?"

"Yes."

"About what, if you can tell me?"

"I drink."

"Oh, one of those. Name please."

"Prester," Digger said. "One of what?"

"Drinkers," she said. "There are a lot of drinkers." There was no apology in her voice at all, and Digger decided the woman had all the natural warmth of a whorehouse madam. This was no Jane Block. Too bad. He wondered whether her coldness was natural or the result of the good reverend's admonishments.

"Is that your last name or your first name?"

"Last name. First name's John. Prester, comma, John," Digger said.

She wrote it neatly that way on the file folder. From inside the folder, she took a printed sheet of paper and wrote that information on it also. She

asked Digger his address and when he gave her his
Las Vegas address, she asked what he was doing in
Florida.

"I'm on vacation. With my girl friend. We're
living in sin. Should I tell the reverend about it?"

"If you want."

"Can I try it out on you first?"

There was no reaction from her at all. "Next of
kin?" she said.

"None. I'm an orphan."

"Occupation, Mr. Prester?"

"I'm a degenerate gambler. I don't work," he
said.

She seemed to find that no more interesting than
his breast-baring about his immoral sex life.

"Maybe I'm too much for the reverend," Digger
said. "Maybe I shouldn't even be here. It's probably
too late anyway."

She looked at him sharply. "No, you're not too
late. You're early." She glanced at the wall clock.
"Fifteen minutes early."

"You don't think I'm a lost cause?" he asked.

"Please go back outside and wait, Mr. Prester.
The reverend will be with you shortly."

"Thank you. Listen, Miss . . ." He paused but she
volunteered no name. "I don't have a lot of money.
Between gambling and women and liquor, you know
. . . what will this cost me?"

"There is no charge," she said crisply. "The
Reverend Wardell does not ask a fee for bringing
sinners to God." The statement sounded like a
scolding.

Digger mumbled "Thank You." He returned to
the waiting room but was seated only several minutes before the door opened again and the blonde
said, "The reverend will see you now."

She waited in the doorway for him but drew back

sharply as he walked past her, clearing her bosom only by inches.

"First door on the left," she said. "Go right in, he's expecting you."

Damien Wardell was sitting behind his desk when Digger entered. He wore reading glasses perched on the end of his nose and he pushed them back atop his blond hair when he rose to greet Digger.

The study was a large and comfortable room, its walls lined with bookshelves. The desk was piled high with a half-dozen books and Wardell had been writing with a fountain pen on a yellow, legal-sized pad. A Bible was open on the desk and alongside it, Digger could see the manila file folder with his name on it. Prester, John.

Wardell was smaller than he had appeared on the stage, but his handshake was firm and his eyes, electric blue, seemed to rivet themselves to Digger's.

"Sit down, Mr. Prester. Coffee?" he asked.

"Please."

Wardell walked to an electric pot on a shelf in the corner and began to pour two cups. "I love coffee," he said. "Thank heavens, there's no biblical proscription against it."

Here, in the room, the voice was softer and muted but it still seemed to hint of the power it displayed on stage.

"Accident of time," Digger said. "Coffee came after the Bible. If it had been around then, there would have been a prohibition, count on it."

Wardell turned away from the coffeepot and smiled.

"Judging from your accent, that sounds like a cynical New York view of the Bible," he said.

"Not really. But I read Leviticus when I was a kid. You can't eat a hawk but you can eat a grasshopper. If it's got four legs, but two of them are above the

122

other two, then you can eat it. Unless it creeps, then you can't eat it. And if you get a white spot on your skin, well, you're all right, unless the spot is lower than your skin and your hair turns white, then you've got leprosy, and you can't wear wool, unless your skin is green, except if you bought a house and the owner wants to reclaim it inside a year, then there's a different rule. Black, please."

He looked at Wardell for a reaction but there was none. He was beginning to get the feeling that he was dealing with zombies and if he had ripped off his clothes and danced naked in their parking lot, they would have said, "That's nice, but be sure to stop before winter, because it gets chilly then."

Wardell brought back the two cups of coffee. He set one on a paper napkin in front of Digger and put the other on his desk blotter. Still standing, he glanced at Digger's file, then walked to the wall bookshelves.

"You don't look like an alcoholic," he said over his shoulder. "And you don't talk like one."

"I drink like one," Digger said. He watched Wardell pull a book from a shelf and begin thumbing through it.

"How much do you drink?" Wardell asked.

The question had never occurred to Digger before. He thought quickly. "I don't know. A quart a day?"

"That's terrible. Do you know what you're doing to your body?"

"Preserving it against the cold?"

"Destroying it for now and eternity," Wardell said. No humor, Digger decided. The place was as full of laughs as a high mass.

"What is it you want me to do?" Wardell asked.

"I had heard you had some experience and success in dealing with alcoholics," Digger said.

Wardell came back to his desk holding a book, sat down and sipped noisily at his coffee. "But they have to want to change, they have to want to put themselves totally in my hands. I don't think that applies to you."

"Perhaps not," Digger said. He heard another voice. It was a woman's voice, singing, and the voice was pure and clear. It had to be Wardell's wife's, but she was singing "A Foggy Day in London Town" and her voice was teasing the song, playing with the melody, in a way that belonged in a recording studio, not a rectory.

"My wife," Wardell said. "She sings. No, I don't think you want to change, if there is indeed anything at all to change. I don't even think that's why you came here. So why don't you tell me who you are and what you want?"

"What do you mean?" Digger asked.

Wardell looked down at the book on his desk, lowered his glasses to his eyes and began to read aloud.

"Prester John. A fabled medieval Christian king of the Orient, supposedly descended from the Magi. His legend arose about the twelfth century. His realm originally was supposed to be located in India but later became centered around Abyssinia. While the story may have had some factual nucleus, it quickly became overlaid by magic and marvels. The legend of Prester John was brought to the West by the contact with the East brought about by the Crusades."

"Didn't fool you for a minute, did I?" Digger asked.

"No, sir. I know my church history."

"Sorry," Digger said. "Just a little joke. Your secretary looked like she could use some humor in her life."

"Secretary . . . oh, Erma. She's a very sedate and reserved young woman. Who are you?"

"The name's Burroughs, Julian Burroughs. I'm with Brokers' Surety Life Insurance Company. I'm looking into the plane accident a couple of weeks ago."

"Oh. You had the plane insured?"

"No. The passengers."

"I see. Terrible accident. Just when I thought that maybe we could change those tragic lives, and then . . . well, God works strangely sometimes."

"You knew the victims?" Digger asked.

"Of course. They were part of our flock. All of them had come here for counseling."

"They were a pretty seedy lot," Digger said.

Wardell shook his head. "The shepherd worries about his lost sheep more than those that are safe in the fold. I thought we could help."

"Why Puerto Rico?" Digger asked.

"It was something new we were trying. We thought if we could get them out of this environment into one that was totally new to them, one that we controlled, we might have a better chance of turning them around."

"You say 'we.' Who's we?"

"All of us. Me. Candace. That's Sister Wardell. Erma. The rest of our staff. But I don't understand, Mr. Burroughs, exactly what your concern is and why you came here under a false name and false pretenses. Why didn't you just come over as what you are?"

"I wanted to get a look at you first."

"Why?"

"Because it isn't every day that I meet someone who's been left six million dollars in insurance."

The coffee cup stopped halfway to Wardell's mouth.

"What?" he said. Digger knew immediately that his shock was genuine.

There was silence for a moment, filled faintly with the sound of Candace Wardell singing. She was doing Rodgers and Hart now, "There's a Small Hotel." With six million, she could buy her own hotel. A big one.

"Six million dollars. That's what you've been left."

Wardell looked amused at having a madman in his study, then astonished when he saw Digger was not joking.

He picked up his telephone and dialed two digits. Abruptly, the singing stopped.

"Candace, come in here," Wardell said brusquely.

A moment later, Mrs. Wardell walked in through a side door. She was dressed like a twin with Erma, the secretary, in white jeans and a light blue blouse. Was this the church uniform? She looked at Digger questioningly for a moment, then at her husband.

"Yes, Damien?"

"This gentleman is Mr. Burroughs. He's with an insurance company. He said the church has been left six million dollars because of the plane crash."

"Not the church," Digger said. "You. All the passengers made out insurance policies with you personally as beneficiary. Forty people. Thirty-nine passengers and the pilot, a hundred and fifty thousand dollars each. That's six million."

Digger was watching Candace Wardell. She was staring at him, but he could not read the look on her face. Was it astonishment? Or just some kind of greedy anticipation?

"My goodness," she said.

"Did you know the passengers were going to do that, make insurance out to me?"

"No," she said. She shook her head for emphasis and said it again. "No." She was overly deferential with her husband, Digger thought. It would not have been hard to imagine her standing there, trembling.

"All right," he said. "You can go now."

"Yes, Damien," she said submissively. Without even looking at Digger, she went back out the door. He noticed that she had broken the symmetry of her costuming. Erma, the secretary, had a blue handkerchief stuck into her left rear jeans pocket. Mrs. Wardell carried a red handkerchief in her right pocket. Digger smiled ruefully to himself and thought that while these women were sure more fun to watch than nuns they weren't a hell of a lot more entertaining. The door closed softly behind Mrs. Wardell.

"Well, Mr. Burroughs," Wardell said. "What's next?"

"Do you have any idea why that plane crashed?"

"Why would I have . . ." He paused. "You don't believe, you can't believe that I . . . for insurance money, that I had anything to . . ."

"I don't believe or disbelieve anything," Digger said. "I'm just checking into things, and you can guess how my job is, I have to look into everything. For instance, the pilot of the plane."

"Steve? Steve was one of us."

"How do you mean that?" Digger asked.

"When he first came to us, he had just quit drinking and he didn't think he'd have the strength to stay sober. We worked with him and God gave him strength to overcome his problem."

"He named you as beneficiary, too," Digger said.

"Maybe, Mr. Burroughs, you find this all suspicious. But let me tell you, that I'm touched. The thought that all these poor people, that they thought enough of me. . . . Well, I'm touched."

"Not as touched as we are. We're being touched for six million," Digger said.

"I think you should leave, Mr. Burroughs. I resent your implications and I think, if you have anything further to say to me, you might talk to my attorney."

It was a cold, flat dismissal and Digger left. But before he reached the door to the waiting room, he heard a sound and turned. Candace Wardell was standing in a partially opened doorway down the hall, gesturing for him to join her.

He followed her into the room, a small study, with a piano against one wall, a small desk against another.

She closed the door behind him.

"I heard you practicing," Digger said. "You don't sing like that in church."

"No. Our folks like their music straight," she said. "Sit down," she said. Digger sat, thinking that while she might be afraid of her husband, she was certainly not afraid of Digger. "Sit down" had been an order, not an invitation.

"Is that all true?" she said. "What my husband said?"

"Yes."

"Six million dollars?"

"Yes," he said. "Give or take a couple of hundred thou. All made out to your husband as beneficiary."

"That's weird," she said. Her soft blond hair was framed foggily about her face in the glare of light from the room's only window. Digger saw that the window opened onto the parking lot behind the rectory.

"You didn't know anything about it?" Digger said.

"No, not a thing."

"It just seems odd that a whole planeload of

people would have decided to do something like that, and you wouldn't even have a clue."

"Mister Burroughs. I'm sorry, for your company, but I'm sorrier for those losers who died." She was about to say more but the door burst open.

"Dacey dear," said Erma who bustled into the doorway. "I . . ." She saw Digger and stopped.

"Not now, Ninde. Later," Mrs. Wardell said.

"Sorry. I didn't know you were . . ."

"Later," Mrs. Wardell said sharply.

The young blonde left. Digger thought that while Candace might jump when her husband barked, she knew how to bark herself.

"Did you charter the plane for the flight?" Digger asked.

"Yes. I asked Erma to do it, but she's not much on bargaining."

"What do you mean 'bargaining?'"

"Bargaining," she repeated. "We were paying the cost of this flight. The people who were going didn't have any money so we were paying for everything and we wanted to get the best price."

"Where were they going in Puerto Rico?" Digger asked.

"A little town up in the hills. Cidra. There's a building there we were going to use. An old mansion. We had hired some staff and everything."

"I'm sorry it didn't work," Digger said.

"I am, too. Damien really wanted to do something for those people."

"He did," Digger said.

"Yes?"

"Yeah. He got them killed."

"That isn't kind," Mrs. Wardell said. She looked out the window at the parking lot. "You say there's how much insurance?"

"Six million. My company looks into it and if it's on the up and up we pay. Unless there's some kind of court action or something that could tie it up."

"Court action?"

"You know. There are all kinds of possibilities. Like other potential beneficiaries. Take Mrs. Donnelly, the pilot's wife. You remember him, don't you?"

"Yes. He came here frequently. What about Mrs. Donnelly?"

"She's all bent out of shape because she wasn't his beneficiary. She might just sue to get her hands on some of that insurance money."

Mrs. Wardell nodded thoughtfully. "I see," she said.

"Did the passengers just meet at the airport?" Digger asked.

"No. They met here and went by bus."

Just then, the door to the room opened again, and a tall, genial-looking, red-haired man walked in. "Candace," he said, "Damien just told me about . . ." He stopped when he saw Digger.

"Jack, come on in," Mrs, Wardell said. Mister Burroughs, this is Jack Thomasen, our accountant." The man looked at Digger with almost a territorial interest. "Mister Burroughs is with the insurance company."

"I see. Nice to meet you, Burroughs." He shook Digger's hand, squeezing.

"Mister Burroughs just told us that there is some insurance money on the plane."

"I know. Damien told me. We'll discuss it later. So long, Burroughs." He had made the word "later" sound dirty.

Digger nodded and when the man left, he rose from his chair.

"Thank you for your time," she said.

"My pleasure."

"We don't get many music lovers here," she said.

"Call me when you book your concert tour."

She smiled, opened the door of the room and stood in the doorway watching him until he went out into the waiting room, where four people now sat on sofas waiting for the Reverend Wardell.

On the front steps, Digger lit a cigarette, then darted alongside the house to the window of the room he had just been in. He peeked inside through the slit between the curtain and the window frame and saw Jack Thomasen enter the room, and happily slap his hand on Candace Wardell's shoulder. Then he clapped his hands together in an obvious display of glee.

Candace looked glum. She said a few words and Thomasen, the smile vanishing from his face as rapidly as the look of pain from a baby's face, turned and left the room. Mrs. Wardell looked up a number in the telephone book and picked up the telephone on the desk in front of her.

She dialed and then began to speak. But the windows were tightly closed and Digger could not hear what she was saying.

He wished he knew who she was talking to.

Koko was not in their room when Digger returned. He called New York.

As she always did, Walter Brackler's secretary said, "Julian Burroughs?"

"Yes. Julian Burroughs. The same name I always give when I call."

"I'll see . . ."

"I know, you'll see if he's in. He's in. Where would he be except in the office? Who would allow him anywhere else? Just put him on the line."

It was no use.

"Just a moment, sir. I'll see if he's in."

Digger hoped she was good looking because that girl was going no place on her brains. The random thought occurred to him that maybe Brackler was sleeping with her, but he put it out of his mind as preposterous. Not Watler Brackler. Not Kwash, all five feet of him, all slick-back hair of him, all cheap suit of him. No. Preposterous.

"Hello, Burroughs?"

"Kwash, are you hitting that chick?"

"What are you talking about?"

"Your secretary. You banging that?"

"You're disgusting."

"Sight unseen, so is she probably," Digger said.

"Eat your heart out. She's a beauty."

"I'll believe it when I see it. Listen, there's a religious retreat in Cidra in Puerto Rico. It's run by Damien Wardell."

"Yes?"

"See if our guys in Puerto Rico can find out anything about it. Who owns it? What's it for? I'm just scratching around."

"Another waste of time," Brackler said. "I bet you're sunburned."

"Yesterday, I hurt. Today I'm all right."

"Instead of spending your time on the beach, tanning at our expense, you might call in once in a while and let us know what's going on."

"Nothing's going on," Digger said. "Another thing. Those insurance applications? Do you have the originals?"

"Yes. Why?"

"Have somebody look at them. See if the handwriting looks alike."

Brackler sighed. "Am I supposed to hire a handwriting expert for this?"

"No. Just give it to somebody with eyes and brains. They'll be able to tell. Oh, and another thing . . . so far, we've saved you three hundred thousand."

"How'd you do that?"

"First, by finding out that one passenger used a phony address. That should void the policy. The other is by reading the freaking policy. Pilots can't insure themselves that way."

"I'll be . . . of course not."

"I'm ashamed of you, Kwash. Do I have to do everybody's job for them?"

"We would have realized it."

"Sure, sure, sure, sure, sure."

"Your mother has been trying to reach you."

"Did you tell her I was out of town?"

"Yes."

"What else did you tell her?"

"I told her where out of town you were."

"You told her I was here?" Digger said.

"Yes."

"I hate you, Kwash."

After hanging up and pouring himself a drink, Digger finally understood what had been bothering him about Wardell. Today, Erma had told him there was no charge for personal counseling by Reverend Wardell. And there had been no admission charge, when he had gone to see Wardell preach, no passing of the plate. There had not even been a charge for parking in the lot.

And today, Candace Wardell had told him that the church was even paying to charter the airplane that had gone down.

What the hell kind of twentieth-century church was this? Didn't Wardell realize that passing the plate was as central to fundamentalist theology as the infallibility of the Bible as historical record? How did he raise money?

Digger went to the phone to Trini Donnelly. He had dialed half the number when he hung up, and had to think about what name he had given her when he had first gone to see her.

His own name. That was a surprise.

He dialed again and she answered the telephone on the first ring. Her voice sounded bright and happy.

"Trini, this is Julian Burroughs."

Her up turned into an instant down. He could almost hear the corners of her mouth dropping.

"Oh? Yes?"

"I was wondering if I might come over?"

"What for?"

"I don't know. I thought, well, maybe we could have that drink."

"I don't think so, Mr. Burroughs. I'm kind of busy."

"Oh. I see. Well, the telephone's all right. The night of the accident, did you pack your husband's lunch? And the name's Julian."

"He didn't take a lunch."

"He brought coffee."

"He was finicky about coffee. He always made his own. If that's all . . ."

"Just one thing. I wanted to tell you that you really might think about suing over that insurance. I asked my office and they . . ."

"Sue? I think that's kind of ridiculous."

"You said you were thinking about it."

"Just anger talking, Mr. Burroughs. There's nothing to sue about. If Steve wanted his insurance to go to the church, that was his prerogative."

"You didn't feel that way yesterday."

"Times change."

"Well, my company might sue anyway. Hold up all these insurance payments," Digger said. "Get everything out in the open."

"That's up to you. I really have to go, Mr. Burroughs. Good-bye."

"Good-bye, Trini. Give my love to those boys of yours."

Chapter Eighteen

"Mom, this is Julian."

"Julian? Julian who?"

"Your son, Mother. How many Julians do you know who call you Mom?"

"Oh, that Julian. Tall? Blond? Let's make sure we're talking about the same person."

"It's the same person, Mother. The one you kept exiling to summer camp the day public school closed."

"That's not funny, Julian."

"After I escaped I thought it was hilarious."

"I want to talk to you. Can't we talk civil for a change?"

"I'll try. What do you want to talk about?"

"I've been trying to reach you and trying to reach you. I called that number in Las Vegas where you live with that thing but she wasn't there."

"That thing's name is Koko, Mother. You can call her Miss Fanucci if you don't want to get too personal."

"It's not important. Anyway, I kept calling that nice Mr. Brackler. He finally reached you?"

"I knew you'd love Kwash, Mother. Yes, he reached me. What do you want?"

"It's not for myself."

"What? For who?"

"For Cora."

"What does Cora want?"

"I don't know. She doesn't tell me a lot since you left her. She said it was important. Probably something to do with the children. She didn't sound too panicky, though. Probably it's not a *real* emergency."

"I'll call her, Mother. Where is Pop? Is he there?"

"Mister Brackler was nice enough to tell me you were in Fort Lauderdale and then he found out where and I was going to call you. I wasn't about to call every place in Lauderdale."

"No, Mother, of course not. I was counting on that. Is Pop there?"

"I'll get him."

"Thank you."

His mother put the telephone down with all the care and attention that he wished she had lavished on him when he was a boy. His father would be sitting on the enclosed back porch, under the thirteen engraved police citations that attested to his excellence as a New York City policeman before he was put out to pasture. A beer can would be almost totally hidden inside his massive hand as he sat watching the Mets game, talking to the television set, trying by the force of his will to teach clumsy fielders to field and blind batters to hit.

He heard his mother's glass-cutting voice scream.

"Patrick. It's him."

A few seconds later, the telephone was picked up.

"Hello, Digger."

"Hello, Sarge. How's it going?"

"Another grinding day like all days, filled with events that do nothing to alter or illuminate our time. And I have to be there."

"If you had it to do over, Sarge, would you marry again?" Digger asked.

"Once wasn't enough? Would you?"

"I don't know."

"I wouldn't turn my back on that little one so fast."

"Koko?" Digger said.

"She's a sweetheart, sonny."

"I know, Pop. Do you know what Cora wants?"

"Probably to bust your balls. I didn't hear."

"Okay, Sarge. See you when I get back."

"Okay. We'll go get some drinks."

"Since when have you started drinking again?" Digger asked.

"Since I ran out of other excuses to get out of the house."

"Take it easy, Sarge. That way lies death and destruction."

"Here in the house, too," his father said.

"Love ya, Sarge."

"Me, too, son. Throw Koko one for me."

"I'm trying, Pop. I'm trying."

Before calling his ex-wife, Digger had another drink for courage. He hated to talk to her.

In the first few years they had separated, her voice was always reeking with smarmy self-pity about how her life had been ruined and what was there to live for. After a while, that gave way to pure animal hatred of the man who had done her wrong.

But lately, she had become unpredictable as she worked to perfect a new approach. She pitied Digger. She pitied him because he had no wonderful family to care for him. He had no one on whom to lavish his love. How empty his life must be. How sad and pathetic a figure he really was.

He could deal with her self-pity or her hate. Or both. But the new tactic was getting under his craw.

He hoped she would just be vicious and nasty when he called her.

"Hello, Cora."

"Julie? Is this Julie?"

"Why do you sound like Al Jolson when you say that?" Digger asked.

"Ah, yes. It's Julie. The Playboy of the Western World."

"What do you want? And please don't call me Julie."

"Married a dozen years, I can't call you Julie?"

"Divorced for six, you can't. Julian. Mr. Burroughs. Ex. You can call me Ex for ex-husband. I'll call you E for empty."

"I want to talk to you about your children."

"What's-his-name and the girl?"

"How many other children do you have?"

"None that I know of. What about the children?"

"I don't think it's fair that you go off gallivanting, vacationing anywhere you want and those children have to sit up here, waiting for some goddam Fresh Air Fund to take them to summer camp."

"I'll ship up a pound of hot dogs. Have a cookout. Tell them it's summer camp at home."

"No, Julie, that won't work. I think you're down there in Fort Lauderdale, playing in the sun, the least . . ."

"I'm not playing, Cora. I'm working. You know the word?"

"Don't be sarcastic. I think it's about time your children spent some time with you."

"I'll take them to the movies the next time I'm in town. If something good's playing. I'm waiting for *Superman Eighteen*."

"You remember your divorce agreement. It says you are supposed to see them frequently."

"No. It says I'm supposed to see them as frequently as I wish with no interference from you."

"You mean you don't want to see your own kids?"

Digger was silent for a moment. "What do you want, Cora?"

"I've been trying to reach you for God knows how long. I'm driving down to Miami tomorrow, me and the kids. I'm going to leave them with you for a few days."

"No, you're not."

"Yes, I am. It's about time you saw them again."

"I'm working. I don't have time to baby-sit."

"No, I guess you're too busy with your Japanese girlfriends and your stewardesses and your hatcheck girls and all those other things you seem to attract, God knows why."

"A hundred million women can't be wrong."

"I'll be down there day after tomorrow. I'm leaving the kids with you. Julie, it's just for a few days. Don't you think I deserve a vacation once in a while?"

"From what?"

"Goddamit, from these kids. Two days, Julie, we'll be there. They're looking forward to it. I don't know why. Good-bye."

The telephone clicked in his ear and Digger came to the realization that if vodka didn't exist, he would have had to invent it.

He had a drink. The half-gallon bottle was almost empty and he wondered for a moment if Koko were sneaking drinks on him. Some people did that, sneaking drinks the minute your back was turned. They never cared how low the bottle got and they never thought of replacing it with a fresh bottle. Some people were just impossibly heartless and cruel. He weighed that argument against the fact that Koko didn't, couldn't, drink. He was not ready to make any snap decisions of innocence in her behalf. If he did, it would mean he had drunk this whole half-gallon by himself and he doubted that.

Oh, yeah, Koko, I doubt that very much. Maybe she was entertaining heavy-drinking boyfriends while he was out working. That could happen, too.

The telephone rang. It was Koko.

"Listen," Digger said. "I don't have time to talk about your drinking right now."

"What are you talking about?" she said.

"We've got to finish this up fast. My kids are coming to town."

"What's-his-name and the girl?" Koko asked.

"Yeah. The ex is driving them down. She wants me to baby-sit, for Christ's sakes."

"It might be nice to meet them," Koko said.

"Come on. What's-his-name picks his nose. The girl's got braces or something. She always had corn kernels stuck in her braces. I think she sleeps in a corncrib."

"Digger, when the hell was the last time you saw them?"

"What has that got to do with anything?"

"How old are they?" she asked.

"I don't know. He's eleven or something. She's younger. I think."

"Come on, Digger. He's sixteen."

"He can't be."

"He is."

"If he's sixteen, well, then, she's almost something like that," he said.

"I think you ought to see them. I'd like to meet them. You're their father. You ought to try to get close to them. Before their youth vanishes."

"I don't want to see them. I don't care about their youth, I hope *they* vanish. We've got two days to straighten this all out and get out of here before Cora arrives. She's got a special car. It's got screens between the front and back seats so they can't sink their fangs into her neck. And there's no handles on the back doors so they can't escape. I think when she drives she lets them go to the toilet in open fields. She calls them back with one of those special whistles that humans can't hear."

"Digger, you're awful. I bet they're nice, sweet kids."

"Shows how little you know. Two days we've got. That's all."

"Okay, if you're in a hurry, you ought to get down here. I've got something, maybe," she said.

"Where are you?"

"I'm at the . . . excuse me, what is this place?" Digger heard someone mumble in the background. "Arthur's Old Mill. I think that's what the bartender said. It's on Treacy Street."

"Okay, I'll be there in a few minutes. Order me a drink."

"I'll wait for you. You're buying me dinner."

"A quick dinner. We've got to hurry. Only two days," Digger said.

"You know what frightens me?"

"What frightens you, Digger?"

"If what you say is true, and What's-his-name is sixteen, pretty soon he'll be seventeen."

"Yes. That seems so," Koko said.

"And then eighteen and nineteen and so on. That means he'll be driving and then carrying switch-blades and knives and guns and bombs and things and you know his mother has poisoned his vestigial mind against me and he's going to try to kill me."

"Now's the time to make him love you, then," Koko said.

"It's too late. He might even try murder on this trip."

"Work on your daughter, then," Koko suggested.

"It's too late. I'm doomed," Digger said.

"Try not to think of it," Koko said. "Think about this. I checked out the next four people on your list. The same thing, nobodies on their way from noplace to nowhere. No families, no possessions, nothing at all."

"You got me here to tell me that? I should be back in the room trying to find out who's been stealing my vodka."

"The fifth guy, Henry Plesser. He lives around the corner. Lived, that is. He was a little better than the rest. He worked in some hardware store as a clerk. I went to the store, nobody really knew much about him. But he had a neat room in a private house. He paid his rent. He drank too much, but he did it quietly."

"So far sounds just like everybody else," Digger said.

"Yes, but. I talked to his landlady for a while. She's a pain in the ass but she talked. This Plesser was really sick. She said that he told her he was going to die."

"What was he sick with?"

"She didn't know. She guessed cancer or something."

"She know his doctor?"

"No. I asked. Anyway, that's not important. What's important is that she's got a letter from him."

"Why would he write to his landlady?"

"It's not *to* her. It's a letter he gave her to mail just before he left to go on the plane."

"Did she mail it yet?"

"No."

"Who's it to?"

"I don't know. She wouldn't show it to me and she wouldn't give it to me."

"Who'd you tell her you were?" Digger asked.

"I told her I was doing a magazine article on the crash. She looked like a whacko so I told her I was doing a piece on this plane lost in the Bermuda Triangle. All nuts believe in the Bermuda Triangle and she looked like a nut."

"You gave her your real name?"

"No. I told her I was Hannah Honda."

"You're as bad as I am. You sound like a Los Angeles TV newsperson," Digger said.

"Anyway, I thought the letter might be real important."

"It might be," Digger agreed. "As soon as I finish this drink."

"If I ever get on your case again about your lifestyle, I apologize now. This is awful work and I don't know how you do it. I've spent so much time in flophouses in the last three days, I think I've got bug bites on my ankles."

"I'll bite your ankles."

"No thank you. Try that offer on your aging stewardess friends," Koko said.

"Mrs. Birnbaumer?"

"Yes."

"Thank God you're still alive. Let's get inside quick. Off this porch."

Digger brushed by the woman with effort. She was big enough to block the passage through a doorway of a human, a breath of air or a sound.

She turned and closed the door behind him. He was in a living room, whose furniture style told him that flowered fabrics were in forty years ago.

"What is this about?" the woman asked. Digger waved a card under her nose, too close for her to see it.

"Interpol. I'm Edgar Allan Dupin. Believe me, fine lady, I am happy to see you are still well."

"What are you . . . ?"

"Was there a woman here today to see you? A Japanese lady?"

"Yes. A cute little thing. Just a couple of hours ago."

"Madam, lions playing are cute. But woe betide the person who stumbles among them. Just a couple of hours ago, you say?"

"Yes. She left only a couple of hours ago. She was a writer."

"Hmphhh. She *said* she was a writer. The truth, Mrs. Birnbaumer, is that . . . what was the name she used?"

"I don't know. Honda. That's it. I remember thinking it was like the car. Hannah Honda."

"Naturally. She would. There is still time for me to intercept her. Fortunately for you."

"What is this all about?"

"The secret message we intercepted said there was a letter. What letter is that? Did you speak to her of a letter?"

"Yes. One of my roomers. He left a letter. It's over here." She went to the bookshelf where she kept a spiral wire dachshund, its body filled with bills and notes and letters. She pulled out a small white envelope. "He asked me to mail it. He died."

"Thank God you have it. There is still time to head her off. So that your roomer does not have company in death."

"She was nice. What are you talking about?"

"Mrs. Birnbaumer. That woman who called herself Hannah Honda is one of the most insidiously evil criminal minds in the history of the world. The tortures she has inflicted on men are beyond belief. I myself wear the scars of her cruelty. I have spent the last ten years at Interpol tracking her down. Have you ever heard of the Bermuda Triangle?"

"Yes . . . everybody . . . *she* talked about the Bermuda Triangle."

"Of course she did. Many people believe that the Bermuda Triangle is some mystic place filled with strange psychic powers where planes and ships vanish and are never found again."

"That's right."

"But I, Edgar Allan Dupin, am here to tell you that this is not so. No. Every vessel which has vanished in that triangle has vanished because of the evil of the woman you call Hannah Honda. There is a simple explanation for every one of these disappearances. Those planes and boats have been captured by Hannah Honda's agents, their passengers spirited away to, God knows, what kind of living hell. Quick, the letter," he commanded.

Mrs. Birnbaumer lumbered toward the wire dachshund, took the letter and handed it to Digger.

"I will take this, Mrs. Birnbaumer, and send it immediately to Paris for analysis. With it gone from this house, you will be safe. Her anger will be directed at me, Edgar Allan Dupin. Of Interpol." Digger shoved the letter into his pocket and walked toward the door.

He stopped there. "I will see that there will be a man watching this house for the next forty-eight hours, until I am sure I can contact her and let her know that I have the letter, not you. You won't be able to see him but he will, I vow, be able to see you. You understand?"

"Yes. I think so," Mrs. Birnbaumer said.

"I would keep your blinds drawn if I were you. Just for a few days. Hopefully, by then, I will have rid the earth of this evil woman's monstrous shadow."

"My god, Inspector. Thank you."

"It is I who thank you, Madam. With your help,

146

we may yet succeed where hundreds of others have tried and failed." He smiled. "You were one of the lucky ones," he said.

Digger opened the envelope.

"How'd you get it?" Koko asked, fork stopped halfway to her mouth.

"I told her you were responsible for the Bermuda Triangle. That you were also in charge of the Japanese-Italian Triangle but that hasn't been getting much action lately."

"That's what you think," Koko said. "You just think I've been working. What's the letter say?"

"Dear Martha," Digger said. "I'm sorry that I said our mixed marriage wouldn't work. Since that time, I've found out that some men even sleep with Japanese women, although how they can do that is beyond me."

"Prick. Read the letter," Koko said.

"Dear Martha. I'm sorry the way things turned out. It's been a long time, how long, twelve years, but I still think of you a lot, all the time, and never a day goes by that I don't regret what I've done. Anyway, it's too late to cry about spilled milk because there isn't a chance of us ever getting back together the way we were. It's too late for both of us. And specially too late for me. But I'm going to try to do something with myself, something that'll make you think of me a little more kind than you might otherwise without me doing it. You'll be hearing about me and I hope you forgive me for what it was I done. Henry."

He looked up at Koko who was polishing off her steak. While the woman could not drink, she was one of the world's marvelous eaters. She would finish everything she ordered and most of Digger's food, too. She weighed 110 pounds. She would always weigh 110 pounds.

"What do you make of it?" he asked.

Busily chewing, she mumbled, "You first."

"I think he's another Jesus freak, writing this sappy, maudlin letter and then he's going to come back from Puerto Rico and tell her how he learned to walk on water and will she take him back. A lot of bullshit."

"I don't know," she said. "There's a lot of finality about that letter. 'Too late for me.' 'Too late to cry about spilled milk.' I'm not so sure."

Digger looked at the address on the envelope. Miss Martha Buchler in Butler, Pennsylvania. "Hold on a minute," he said.

He left the table, taking the envelope with him. Koko took the occasion to pick at his uneaten salad.

When he came back in ten minutes, his salad bowl was empty.

"Where's my salad?"

"It was wilting. Where'd you go?"

"I called Martha in Butler. This guy was her husband. He left her when she was pregnant twenty years ago. The drunker he got, the more maudlin he got. He used to write a lot but he never came back to see her. She said he was a lush and a reprobate and she never wanted to hear of him again in her life."

"She hadn't seen him in twenty years?"

"Not since he left her with the brat. I told her he was dead and she said good. She also said he was always writing stupid letters. She threw them away without reading them."

"Anything else?"

"She invited me for dinner the next time I'm in

Butler. I might go. There isn't much else to do in Butler."

"You got a lot accomplished in one telephone call," Koko said.

"I'm good at it. Even though I hate the phone," he said.

"You're always on it," she said.

"Only 'cause I have to be. Some people like talking on the phone but I hate it. I always hope nobody ever calls me. A lot of people aren't like that, though. They like calls. I was driving once on this highway in Connecticut and I bought this cup of coffee in a cardboard container from a machine. Well, on the side of the container they had the name of the company that made it and the phone number. Now, why would they put their phone number on the container, I wondered. I figured they wanted somebody to call. So I call the number and when I got the switchboard operator, I told her I just called to say that they made a really fine cardboard container and they were to be congratulated. Well, she made me hang on and I had to tell the same thing to everybody and everybody and finally I wound up talking to the president of the company and I told him that I really enjoyed his cardboard coffee container. And he wanted to send me a case of cardboard coffee containers and I wouldn't take them and finally he asked me, why'd I call. I was getting mad so I said because you put your freaking number on the container and if you didn't want people to call, why did you do that? Well, a year later, I stopped on that same road for coffee again and this time they took the phone number off the container. Instead, they put on the address of the company."

"So?"

"So I figured they wanted somebody to write

them, so I wrote them a letter and told them they made a really good container, and they sent me a free box of cardboard coffee containers. I give up."

"You're nuts, Digger."

"I think if people give out their phone number, they want to be called. That's why I always call numbers that you find on bathroom walls. For really good head call oh-oh-oh-oh-oh-oh-oh."

"Who do you get when you call?"

"Usually some arithmetic teacher with a student who thinks it's funny to write her name on walls. Once I got a hooker, though."

"What about her?"

"She gave really good head."

"How'd her number get on the wall?" Koko asked.

"She used to give a couple of bucks to this guy who worked in a maintenance service and he wrote her name on walls all over. It pays to advertise, I guess."

He looked at her and said, "Let's go home."

"Yes."

"And make love."

"No," she said.

Chapter Nineteen

DIGGER'S LOG:
Tape recording number four, midnight Friday, Julian Burroughs in the matter of Interworld Airways crash.

If you were an airplane, why would you go down? Don't tell me if you found a pretty lady airplane. That's ridiculous.

No, you'd go down because of a bomb, quite likely. Or mechanical failure. Or pilot error. But Steven Donnelly, sobersided, industrious, God-loving Steven Donnelly doesn't make pilot errors, except to take off without his co-pilot and stewardess. The equipment could fail. That's for sure. Interworld's equipment could fail while it was being gassed up. But unless and until there's wreckage, no one will ever be able to tell.

The problem with those two scenarios is that they don't give any justification for fraud and swindle and I deal in fraud and swindle. It goes this way in my head as a most-likely case. Brother Damien talks the passengers into insuring themselves in his name. Then Brother Damien plants something aboard to bring the plane down.

There's a problem with that. Suppose Randy Batchelor wanted Donnelly out of the way because Donnelly was going to blow a whistle on him. That wouldn't have anything to do with Damien Wardell, though, and I am just not ready to write this all off as coincidence, with all that money going to Wardell, no matter how much I dislike Batchelor.

A bomb. Who brings it on? A passenger? Maybe inside the passenger's luggage. Maybe Donnelly brought it aboard. Or Batchelor. Maybe Batchelor brought on his bomb-laden bag, hung it up, then faked sick to get off the plane. Nobody checks crew when they carry their crap on a plane.

I don't know, goddamit, I don't know. I hate not knowing.

In the master file is another tape, re interviews today with Dr. Richard Josephson, Damien Wardell, Candace Wardell, and a Mrs. Birnbaumer.

Josephson keeps Donnelly's records in a file cabinet alongside his desk. But he won't talk. He told me that and he told the other insurance man. Mustache, dark hair, nice looking, that sounds like Randy Batchelor to me, but what the hell is he doing involved in this? What is he after? What is he afraid I'll find? And why weren't Donnelly's medical records in the Interworld files the first time Jane looked? And then back where they belonged the next day.

And then there is the Wardell ménage. There is Candace, Mother Wardell, who sings like a zombie on stage but is jazz-in-jeans around the digs. And then there's the matching bookend, Erma, the secretary. What did Mrs. Wardell call her? Ninde? What the hell kind of name is that? And weren't they cute? Two big pretty blondes with their matching jeans and blouses and their little handkerchiefs.

Ninde had me fill out a form before my consultation with Wardell. She's got no sense of humor. She didn't recognize the name Prester John. But no charge for the consultation.

I also met Jack Thomasen, Wardell's accountant.

He seemed very happy at having six million pumped into their accounts. Who wouldn't be? And that pat on Mrs. Wardell's shoulder was a little warmer than I would have expected in a rectory. Is he the man who makes Candy sing so passionately? Any electricity between Candace and her husband is negative.

I think I've got a handle on Wardell. He may be sincere, he may be the greatest thing in Evangelism since the hand-held microphone, but I think he's a power junkie. He operates his place like a petty martinet, barking out orders to the wife as if she were a slow-witted janitor. I can see him ordering people to restructure their lives and put themselves into his hands. Even though he knew I was a fake, he couldn't resist talking about the need of people to put themselves "totally in his hands." But he seemed honestly surprised by the six million in insurance. I was watching those narrow little eyes carefully and he didn't know about it. Or he's a better actor than I thought he was. Anyway, there's no sign that they've been spending a lot of money recently.

Kwash is checking out the Puerto Rican retreat and we'll see what that's about. And he's also checking on the handwriting on those insurance applications.

No one knows anything about the insurance and that's a surprise to me because I looked at the insurance form Koko picked up at the airport, and what you do, is you fill it out and then stick it into the machine with your quarters and it snips off the original part of the application, but the rest of the form comes back and it's a self-sealing envelope and you're supposed to put a stamp on it and dump it in the mail. Knowing how ethical and honest all insurance companies are, you have to do that, otherwise the beneficiary could never know he was the beneficiary and America's insurance companies might decide not to pay off if no one knew they had to.

So Wardell should have gotten forty pieces of mail, duplicates of the insurance policies. And they say they didn't get any. So where the hell are they? Who were they mailed to? Were all the passengers so dopey they just stuck the beneficiary's copy of the policy in their pockets when they went on the plane? Some of them had to have read the instructions.

I told Candace that Mrs. Donnelly was thinking of suing. And then Candace was talking on the telephone and I don't know who she was talking to, but later Trini Donnelly wouldn't hear any talk of suing. That's a fast, unexplained change of heart and I think I know who Candace called on the phone.

And then there's Henry Plesser, another of the passengers, whose letter I got from landlady, Mrs. Birnbaumer. Some people will do anything to avoid getting swallowed up in the Bermuda Triangle. What Henry had done was leave his wife and think later he had made a mistake. That tells you Henry was a loser. Probably the only right thing he ever did in his life was leave his wife.

A Jesus-saves letter from somebody gone to take the cure. Koko thinks maybe not, but I just can't see anything substantial in that letter at all.

What did Koko say? My sweet, tired, sleeping-in-armor Koko? She said these guys were nobodies on their way from nowhere to noplace. So am I. I don't know what to do next with this goddam case. I'll think of something. I have to think of something. Any minute now, those two gorilla kids, What's-his-name and the girl, are going to be lashed into Cora's car and start down here. I've got to get done and done fast, otherwise I'll have to see them all again.

Frank Stevens, our president, I love you and honor you. Kwash, I tolerate you. But before meeting with those kids, I will leave here case unclosed. And that's it. Roma Locuta Est.

I'm going to have to put Koko in for a bonus. She's saved the company three hundred thou so far. Who knows? She might get to like this work. Anybody can lie on the beach and get tan but it takes brains to be an insurance investigator.

Expenses today and yesterday. Breakfast in our room, Koko and me, fourteen dollars. Cheese Danish would have been cheaper. Beach. Miscellaneous costs. Ten dollars. That's yesterday. Today. Gasoline for car, twenty-four dollars. Telephone calls, two dollars. Dinner with Koko on the Mrs. Birnbaumer interview, seventy-one dollars. Total, two days, one hundred twenty-one dollars. Make it one-thirty because I'm sure there's some stuff I've forgotten. Koko's taking care of her own expenses. Room and car by credit card.

Chapter Twenty

"I didn't ask for a wake-up call."

"Burroughs, this is Walter Brackler."

"I stand by my previous statement," Digger said. He reached for the lamp, then remembered Koko sleeping next to him. He fumbled around in the dark until he found his cigarettes and lit one.

"We've gotten some word on that Puerto Rican property."

"Shoot."

"It's owned by Damien Wardell. It has been for twenty-five years," Brackler said.

"It can't have been," Digger said. He rolled on his side and talked softly into the phone so as not to wake up Koko who was stirring in her sleep.

"Why not?"

"Wardell's still a young man. Twenty-five years ago, he would have been just a kid."

"A very rich kid, though. In case you don't know it, and the fact that you don't doesn't surprise me, Wardell is the heir of the Wardell Paint Manufacturing Company, which may just be the world's largest. He's owned that property for twenty-five years."

"Okay," Digger said. "If Rockefeller could own Venezuela when he was a kid, I guess Wardell could own a piece of P.R. Anything on those applications?"

"I looked at them myself," Brackler said. "They

don't look like they were all written in the same handwriting. But maybe two or three different handwritings, that was all."

"But not forty different handwritings?" Digger said.

"No. No way."

"Good," Digger said.

"What are you up to down there?"

"Plugging away," Digger said.

"I wish you'd keep in touch and let us know what's going on. It wouldn't hurt if I had some input in your work."

"The reason I don't let you have any input," Digger said, "is that you don't have anything to put in."

"Get to work," Brackler said sourly and hung up.

Digger hung up the phone and slid quietly out of bed.

Where would they be now? With luck, Cora would oversleep and the menagerie might not yet be on its way to Florida. Maybe she'd have car trouble. But there was no sense in hoping for the best. One had to plan for the worst.

After dressing, he wrote Koko a note outlining instructions and left it on the table next to her head before leaving.

On impulse, he stopped for breakfast, wondering why he was hungry before he remembered that Koko had eaten almost his entire dinner the night before. He had eggs and sausage and grits and fresh-baked rolls and coffee. Digger had this deep gut feeling that everybody south of the Mason-Dixon line was a semi-simian shitkicker with a single-digit IQ. But he had to admit, they knew how to eat breakfast.

He bought two containers of coffee to take with him.

It had rained during the early morning hours and when Digger turned onto Galaxy Avenue, he saw the two boys, Spazz and Tard, sitting on the curb in front of their home, throwing stones at passing cars. He zipped in quickly to the curb, through a puddle, splashing them both with water.

"Hey," the bigger one yelled.

"Shit," the smaller one said.

"Hello, you little darlings," Digger said cheerily. It was always nice to start the day by doing good.

He rang the doorbell a long time before Mrs. Donnelly answered. She was wearing a robe and yesterday's makeup.

She looked at him hard for a moment as if trying to place him.

"Julian Burroughs," he said. "Just in the neighborhood, thought I'd stop by with coffee."

He held the bag forward. She looked at it with distaste, before nodding and opening the screen door to let him inside.

"There aren't any eggs in the house," she said. "I can make toast."

"Not on my account," Digger said. "I never eat breakfast."

"Fine. We'll just have coffee. She poured the coffee from the containers into two stoneware mugs and put them on the table in the kitchen. Digger noticed that his read Trini. Hers read Steve.

"If you're here to talk about my suing, forget it," she said. She put a lot of sugar and cream in her coffee. Digger waved it off. He drank his black.

"How come?"

"I thought about it," she said, "and it just didn't seem like it would be worth the bother. It's a shame, but I guess my husband had the right to make insurance out to anybody he wanted."

"Unless he was coerced into doing it," Digger said.

"You think that happened?"

"I don't know. I was talking to Mrs. . . . what's her name?"

"Wardell."

"Yeah, Wardell. Thank you. And she said they didn't know anything about the insurance but I don't know if I believe them. I've talked to my home office and they'll do what I tell them. I think I may tell them not to pay anything. Sue, stall, or something."

"Sue about what?"

"Who knows? Fraud or something. We'll see." He noticed that she was touching his hand again as he spoke. He extricated his hand, got up and went to the counter where he poured some of the coffee remaining in the containers into his cup.

When he walked back to the table, he put his hand on Mrs. Donnelly's shoulder, his thumb touching her bare neck. She squirmed her head back a little, pressing against his hand.

"That feels good in the morning," she said.

"Feels good all the time," Digger said.

"You know what I think?" she asked.

"No, what?"

"What I think is that you should just tell your company to pay off and let it go at that. I talked to Randy yesterday. He stopped by just to say hello and see how I was. He said the accident was just one of those things."

"That all he said?"

"Ah, he just wanted to chitchat. Talk about Steve. How good he'd been. How healthy, yap yap yap. How sorry he was." She squirmed again against his hand. "Let your company pay."

"I'd like to, little girl. But that's not the way I work. I've got my standards."

She stood up and faced him. She put her arms around his waist and he lifted them draping them over his shoulders.

"Can I convince you?" She moved her face forward to be kissed and Digger kissed her. Her tongue darted into his mouth and she pressed her body against his.

"You know, my son was right. We is gonna fuck," she said softly.

Digger thought of the tape recorder whirring smoothly against his back. Taking it off was such a pain in the ass.

"Tonight," he said. "Let's try for tonight. Maybe we can get dinner and then . . ."

"And then what?"

"We'll see what happens," Digger said. "I'll call."

He held her closely so that she would not put her arms around his waist, kissed her again, then backed away from her.

"I'll call," he said. "Let's see if we can connect."

"I hope so," she said.

She walked him to the door, her hand in his. She tilted her head up again to be kissed one more time. Digger leaned forward to her.

"When you talked to Mrs. Wardell," Digger said, "did she say when the insurance might pay off?"

"No. She . . ." Mrs. Donnelly caught herself but it was too late. The warm glow on her face turned to ice. She glared at Digger who shrugged: "Just doing my job, ma'am," he said.

"Get out of here."

"I guess this means dinner is off?"

"Get out of here."

Digger met Koko in a small oceanside restaurant on the ground floor of one of the giant condominium towers that fouled the Lauderdale skyline. When he arrived, she was attacking a sink-sized bowl of seafood salad.

She gulped a hurried swallow and said, "What have you been doing while I've been working my little tits off?"

"Taking advantage of some poor lady with a drinking problem," Digger said.

"Don't tell me about it."

"All right, I will. After I talked to Mrs. Wardell and told her that the pilot's wife might sue about the insurance, she called the wife. And the wife backed off. Now, she's only doing that for money, but why should Wardell care if she sues or not? And Randy Batchelor, who doesn't like her, he went to visit Mrs. Donnelly. He was pumping but I don't know for what. I've let her know that old Benevolent and Saintly might sue about the policies anyway."

"Why'd you say that? The company wouldn't do that."

"I know. I just did it to stir the pot."

"And put yourself in it," she said.

Digger nodded. "Sometimes it's what you've got to do."

He finished his drink and signaled for another.

"Digger, why don't you stop drinking?"

"Because I'm an alcoholic."

"Alcoholics stop drinking all the time. Did you ever think of quitting?"

"I thought of it once. Just the thought gave me the shakes and I hid out in a saloon until it passed."

"This isn't funny. You're going to kill yourself."

"Christ, I hope so."

He looked at her and saw a twinge of hurt in her eyes and he felt himself a shit for having put that there.

"You need a hobby," she said. "Something to replace drinking."

"I was working on it. I thought making love to you might fill the bill but that avenue is closed to me. Unlike you, saloons are always open. Do you know that somewhere, someplace, it is always happy hour?"

"I'm sorry, Digger. I just wish there was something I could do."

"You're doing it," he said. "Help me clean this thing up before those kids and their mother arrive in town."

"What's she like?"

"Your normal run of the mill ex-wife. Castrating iron for a tongue. Her voice shatters Memorex Tape. Suspicious and narrow-minded."

"Is she pretty?"

"I don't know. I never looked."

"Come on, Digger, you were married for more than ten years."

"Eleven and one-twelfth," he said, "but who counts? She's all right looking, I guess. Actually, she was kind of pretty, especially if you get off on fangs. What'd you find out about Wardell?"

Koko's face brightened visibly. She reached beneath the table for her purse, whose straps she had twisted around her ankle, proving that she was an original New Yorker and feared a purse-snatching even in this restaurant peopled solely by retired octogenarian dentists, doctors, rabbis and their wives.

She opened the bag on the edge of the table.

"The library was full of him," she said. She pulled out a sheaf of photocopied clippings which she placed neatly on the table, then closed her purse and put it back on the floor, her foot securely through the straps again. She handed the clippings to him and he glanced at them while she spoke.

"He and two brothers inherited the Wardell Paint Company from their father, who started it. It's not Three-M but it's not a neighborhood candy store, either. Wardell sold out his share to his brothers about five years ago, the *Times* said, for four million dollars. He kept the property in Puerto Rico because that was a gift from his father when he was a kid. Anyway, he took the money from the sale of the business and put it into a trust fund to finance the church down here. The newspapers had a field day with it, how he always wanted to be an evangelist and so forth. *People* magazine did a piece, 'From Profits to Prophecy.' They've done some follow-ups on him. The church runs at a loss because he won't shill bibles or pass the plate or what have you, but it's got to be pretty solid because all the money that trust fund makes should help support it."

"Personal money troubles?" Digger asked.

"Maybe," Koko said. "But none of the stories got too much into that, just talked about how unusual he was in running a free church in this age of religious hucksterism. But he went the whole route. He and his wife took vows of poverty."

"His wife's in the clippings?"

"Yeah. They've been married, I don't know, six or seven years. The former Candace von Schlegel. She was in college, some kind of homecoming beauty queen, majoring in musical theater. Her family didn't have any money, so she probably figured she had plucked the golden goose. When he packed in the paint business, she was interviewed and she said something like her husband would follow the Lord and she would follow her husband. One thing was interesting. She said she had signed a waiver never to make a claim against the church in the event of divorce or anything like that."

"I wonder how she likes being poor?" Digger said.

His face shielded by wide wraparound sunglasses, Digger sat on the thinly padded seat and wished for a cigarette. He resented offices that didn't provide ashtrays for visitors. America had started to go to hell when they took spittoons out of taverns, allowed women in the Clam Broth House in Hoboken, and took ashtrays out of doctors' offices.

Digger glanced at the three other people in the waiting room. All were women. One had a bright red, runny nose and Digger commended his own foresight in having had a liquid lunch so he was fortified with antifreeze to stave off the common cold virus. Another woman's illness was obviously fatness. The third kept scratching her scalp.

The nurse was almost as tall as Digger and her shoulders were wider. Digger thought he might once have seen her in a six-man tag team wrestling match—her against five men. She was sitting behind a counter high enough so that only the top of her head and her eyes were visible to the people in the waiting room. The eyes were cold steel as she glared around the room, probably ensuring that no one was lighting up a forbidden cigarette.

Digger waited until her laser beam eyes were off him, then he fell forward off the bench onto the floor and groaned.

"What's the matter?" asked the woman who kept scratching her head.

"Oooooh," Digger moaned. He held both hands on his stomach and curled up into a fetal position.

"Nurse, you better help," said itchy scalp.

The Fabulous Moolah came out from behind her wall and lumbered over to Digger. She stood over him, staring down, a concentration camp version of Florence Nightingale in her starched whites.

"What's the matter with you?" she demanded.

"Ooooooh," Digger said.

"Hmphhh," the nurse grunted in disgust. "I'll get the doctor."

She knocked on the doctor's office door. A few seconds later, Doctor Josephson opened it.

"Sick man over here," she said.

The doctor squatted alongside Digger.

"What's the matter?"

"Stomach hurts," Digger said.

"Where?"

"In the middle. Here." Digger pointed with his index finger to a spot just below his solar plexus.

"Does it hurt here?" Josephson said. He dug his fingers into Digger's lower right side, near the appendix.

"No. It's passing now," Digger said.

"This ever happen to you before?"

"Yes," Digger said. "All the time. It's psychosomatic. It's okay now." He got to his feet. "I feel a lot better now. Really. I feel good."

The doctor looked at him for a few seconds, then said, "Well, sit there and I'll see you next."

"Thank you. I'll be fine."

When Josephson retreated into his office, Digger stood up and brushed himself off, then strolled over to Nurse Guano's desk.

"I'm going out for a cigarette."

She nodded, not even trying to disguise her annoyance at anyone who would disrupt the normal placid routine of her office. Outside, Digger lit a cigarette, then walked around the corner and waited in his rented car.

Koko arrived fifteen minutes later.

"How'd you make out?" Digger asked.

"Got it right here," she said and patted her purse. "And I've got great lungs, according to the doctor."

"You've got great lungs according to me, too."

"Come on, let's get out of here. I feel like I'm in the damned Watergate, waiting for the burglar alarm to sound."

"All right," Digger said as he drove away. "One more stop first."

Timothy Baker was in the outer office, talking to Jane, his eyes blinking, when Digger came in.

"Oh, it's you," Baker said. Jane smiled at Digger.

"Any word yet on your insurance claim?" Digger asked him.

"Not yet. You should know better than me how these bastards make you wait. What is it you want, anyway?"

Jane winked at Digger who nodded slightly to her.

"Just a quick question," Digger told Baker.

"Oh, for Christ's sakes, go ahead. It's amazing how big you guys are with the questions and how small you are when it comes to paying up. Come on inside."

Inside Baker's office, standing between the cardboard boxes and the pile of *Wall Street Journal*s that had now grown to five feet high, Digger asked, "Did Steve Donnelly ever talk to you about quitting?"

"No. Why should he?"

"I don't know," Digger said. "Maybe he might just not want to fly anymore?"

"No," Baker said. "He never said anything like that." His fingers had started to drum on the desktop. "Listen, I'm helping you, right, and one hand washed the other. Can't you do anything to try to get me my money?"

"I'm trying. I promise," Digger said.

"Okay."

Back outside, a man was leaning over Jane Block's desk, trying without much subtlety to look down into her scoop-necked dress. Digger could only see his back.

"Did you see that egg roll outside?" the man was saying.

"What?" Jane asked.

"There is the most beautiful Chinese broad in the world in that car out there. She is grorious."

Jane saw Digger come out of Baker's office, then looked through the office window at Digger's car where Koko sat in the front seat. Jane shook her head and looked at Digger.

"Your supervisor, no doubt," she said.

Digger shrugged. "Some days she looks better than others."

Randy Batchelor turned from Jane's desk to see who she was talking to. "Oh, it's you," he said.

"Haven't seen you since the party," Digger said. "Didn't get a chance to tell you what a good time I had."

"You're awful," Jane told Digger.

Digger walked toward the door. "I'll call," he told Jane.

"Don't bother," she said.

He had gotten only a few steps from the hangar building when Batchelor caught up to him.

"Hold on, I want to talk to you," he said.

Digger turned around. "Sorry I missed you at Mrs. Donnelly's," he said. "And the doctor's. You've been busy."

"We all have," Batchelor said. "I thought you said you were a cop."

"No. *You* said I was a cop. I just told you I was looking into the crash."

"You're an insurance snoop?"

"That's about it," Digger agreed.

"And just what the hell is your name? Lincoln? Or Burroughs?"

"Depends on who you talk to," Digger said. "Why'd you go see Dr. Josephson?"

"Who's he?" Batchelor said.

"Steve Donnelly's doctor."

"Sorry. Don't know the man," Batchelor said. "Well, what have you found out?"

There was something smug about his manner, Digger thought. He knew something but it was clear that he wasn't going to say what.

"Damned little," Digger said. "I don't know why that plane went down but I still think that somebody gave it a push. Maybe somebody with something to hide caused the accident. Maybe somebody who found some way to be off the plane when it took off."

"Hold on," Batchelor said. "You can't . . ."

"I'm not. I'm just thinking out loud."

"Well, don't think like that. It wasn't that way at all."

"What way was it?" Digger asked.

Batchelor smiled, a sly, unwarm smile. "Maybe someday *you'll* tell *me*."

"I hope so," Digger said, "I hope you can live with the answer."

Batchelor walked away and Digger strolled back to his car. Didn't anybody ever get a day off at Interworld Airways? Saturday morning and Baker was working and Jane was working and Batchelor was hanging around. Maybe they were all just waiting for the mail, hoping an insurance check for the lost airplane would arrive.

"Who was that man?" Koko asked as Digger got into the car.

"Batchelor. The co-pilot who stayed home."

"He doesn't like you," Koko said.

"So few people do nowadays," Digger said. "But he likes you just fine. I heard him. He said you were glorious."

"Good taste," Koko said. Digger started the engine and looked over at her. She was busy reading the Donnelly medical file she had just stolen from Dr. Josephson's office.

"Anything interesting in there?" he asked.

"Not yet. Not unless you find something intrinsically interesting in a surgically corrected hernia."

He had gotten only a few blocks from the airport when Koko said, "Oh my, oh my, oh my, oh my."

"What is it?"

"I think Donnelly had cancer."

"Mister Burroughs?"

"Yes."

"This is Doctor Riesner." The voice crackled sharply over the telephone, in sharp contrast with the appearance of the short, tweedy, pipe-smoking man at whose home Digger had left the medical reports a few hours earlier.

"Yes, Doctor. You find out anything?"

"Your man, Mr. Donnelly, has liver cancer. Very advanced, very terminal."

"Had, Doctor. He's already dead."

"Yes. Well, that was to be expected. Those tests and reports were very clear that he would die any day."

"No chance of remission, no last-minute miracle cure?" Digger asked.

"Afraid not, Mr. Burroughs."

"Thanks, Doctor Riesner. I'll be back for the reports tomorrow."

"Where did you get these, anyway?"

"I'll pretend I didn't hear you ask that. Good night, Doctor."

Chapter Twenty-One

DIGGER'S LOG:
Tape recording number five, 10 P.M., Saturday, Julian Burroughs in the matter of Interworld Airways Crash.

Busy, busy, busy, busy. I should have known that a day that started off with a phone call from Kwash was going to be ruined.

Koko's gone. She decided that she ought to go see the Reverend Wardell for herself. The rich Reverend Wardell.

That's all very interesting, a millionaire who walks away from a fortune to go preach the gospel. And he's got a sense of humor. The Church of the Unvarnished Truth. Paid for with his paint millions. He's got style, you've got to admit that.

We have on tape Trini Donnelly, being hung over and seductive and admitting that Mrs. Wardell called her about not suing.

Anyway, I let Mrs. Donnelly know that maybe I was going to tell the company to sue. We'll see what that brings.

There is no tape of my visit to Dr. Josephson's office, where by sheer tenacity and willpower I persuaded him to give me a copy of Steve Donnelly's medical records. Terminal cancer, going to die any day.

Of course, that doesn't have anything to do with

the insurance policy. It was accident insurance. But he could have had an attack or something while flying. I can understand Donnelly wanting to fly to the bitter end, particularly with all those bills he owed, but he doesn't sound like the kind of guy to endanger passengers that way.

The ultimate pilot error is dying at the controls.

I wouldn't put it past Trini to put a bomb on a plane to get rich on insurance. But who kills forty to get one? And she might be a horny drunk, but she's got enough sense to make sure the insurance is made out in her name, even if it were payable, which it's not. She didn't know about that insurance policy at all. I'm sure of that.

Kwash says all the policies were made out in a couple of different handwritings. So who did them? I don't know.

I guess I'm not going to play Tarzan for Interworld Airways' Jane. Too bad. She saw Koko. It's a lot of bullshit about women respecting other women's rights to a man. They don't. But they say they do and it takes awhile for you to get them past that nonsense and I don't have a lot of time to do anything. The Mongol hordes are on the way. Cora, What's-his-name and the girl are probably sleeping now. But then, tomorrow, inexorably, like some goddam glacier crushing everything in its path, they'll be on their way here. I've got to get out before it's too late.

And what is Batchelor doing? First going to see the doctor, then Mrs. Donnelly, pumping, pumping. He goddamit knows something but I don't know what it is. He's a sleaze with his yacht caps and little blue blazers and Clark Gable mustache. I just don't trust him, he's up to no good. He looks like a smuggler to me. Who else gives away cocaine at parties?

I hope Koko gets back soon.

Expenses: breakfast, Mrs. Donnelly and me, twenty-one dollars, the woman's a big eater. Lunch, Koko, thirty dollars. I round all these numbers off to the next lower dollar. I hope you appreciate this, Kwash. Dr. Riesner, who analyzed Donnelly's records for me, will send a bill to B.S.L.I. Room and car by credit card. Total, fifty-one dollars. Another cheap day.

Chapter Twenty-Two

"Well, that was an experience," Koko said. She was wearing blue jeans, a white blouse and white high-heeled shoes, her generation's idea of Saturday night go-to-meeting best.

"What'd you think of His Holiness?" Digger asked.

"Charisma, but he's a nut-case." She walked back and forth along the shabby rug, imitating better than Digger ever could Wardell's speech rhythms, punctuated by the footsteps along the stage. " 'Prosperity is just around the corner. Good health is just around the corner. Happiness is just around the corner.' Digger, this guy's the king of around the corner."

"You think he's a phony?"

"That's the problem. I don't. I think he's on the level and it annoys me. I wanted to be able to come back and tell you, Digger, go get him, it's him, but I can't."

"Me, neither. I don't picture him as the kind of guy to bring down a plane of forty people," Digger said. "I think he's a manipulative power-junkie, but I don't make him a killer."

"Did you hear from the doctor?" Koko asked.

"Yes. Donnelly had cancer. Maybe only days to live."

"All right," she said. "Pilot error. Or maybe pilot incapacitation. Maybe he had a cancer attack. Do

174

people get cancer attacks? Like migraines and menstrual cramps?"

"I think so," Digger said. He got up from the bed and Koko flopped down on the other side of it.

"Well, that's a possibility, then," she said. "It's a lot more possible than your idea that somebody brought the plane down."

"Except," Digger said sourly, as he started to pace the floor of the room.

"Except what?"

"Except for that damned insurance," Digger said. He kicked the closed drawer of the plastic-veneered dresser.

"Easy on the furniture," Koko said. "Unless you got ten dollars to replace it all."

But Digger wasn't listening. He was walking the floor, talking as much to himself as to her.

"Except for that damned insurance," he said again. "Forty passengers on that plane, all with insurance made out to one man, the man who's sending them on the trip. And then the pilot who is terminal turns out to have insurance made out the same way."

Digger kicked the dresser drawer again. The cheap mirror on the dresser rattled against the wall.

"And why does the pilot take off without his crew when the co-pilot conveniently gets sick?" he asked aloud. "And the co-pilot has the look of a hustler or smuggler or something and now he's nosing around, trying to find things out, and I think he'd down every commercial aircraft in the country to get money to buy a bigger Porsche."

Digger gulped the dregs of vodka from his glass. "And then we've got Timothy Baker," he said. "In deep money trouble and that plane going down might just be the best thing that ever happened to him. And the pilot's wife sleeps around, and when she was talking about suing over the insurance, Mrs. Wardell talked her out of it. Why? And how? And the whole plane was a planeful of losers. No family, no friends, no future. If ever a plane was meant to go down, it was this one."

He looked at Koko imploringly. "Except this, except that, except everything. There are too many damn excepts in this case."

She kicked off her shoes and stretched her hands above her head as Digger kicked the dresser one more time.

"This is an awful job you have," she said. "Nothing's ever simple and nothing's ever what it seems to be."

"That's the fun of it," Digger said.

"I know. I like puzzles, too. But just once in a while, don't you wish something was slambang, whammo?"

"The only thing I want to slambang whammo is you," Digger said.

"Fat chance."

Later, they lay in bed with the lights out, Digger smoking his last cigarette of the night, even though smoking in the dark was totally unsatisfying. If you couldn't see the smoke you could barely taste it. That was true of all cigarettes but especially of Digger's low-tar, low-nicotine brand, about which he complained that he had to suck so hard for smoke, his teeth were coming loose.

"Digger," Koko said.

"You know I don't like to talk during my last cigarette. Now I'm going to have to light another one. This is my quiet-thinking cigarette of the day."

"I'm sorry."

"Well, as long as you started, what is it?"

"This probably doesn't mean anything, but you

176

know how Wardell's tent is kind of hooked up to his rectory building or parsonage or whatever they call it."

"Yeah."

"When Wardell was preaching, someone came up the ramp and slipped his wife a note. She got up and left the stage. She went down that ramp. It struck me as odd, her going like that. Anyway, he was preaching and I had heard enough, so when she left, I nipped out the back of the tent and ran around the side to see what she was up to."

"You see anything?"

"She walked into the parsonage. I thought, hell, maybe she had to go to the bathroom. But then I thought of that note that she got. So I waited awhile, and in a couple of minutes, somebody else came out of the house."

"Who was it?"

"Some woman. She had black hair and big knockers. Sunglasses, too. She got into a car and drove out of the lot."

"What kind of a car?"

"Don't interrupt. I had my car parked in the front of the lot and so I got in my car and tried to follow her."

"How'd you make out?"

"I followed her for about a mile to that big fork in the road, you know that six-way intersection with the gas stations and the motels and some cars got between us and I lost her."

"What kind of a car?"

"I drove around the block a few times but I couldn't see her. Then I went back to the tent and the show was just letting out so I drove right home here."

"What kind of a car?" Digger asked.

"Dark color."

"Oh, that helps. That's good. A dark car."

"I don't know what kind of a car. You want me to tell you it was a 1951 Malibu coupe with double-barrel carbs and California headers and mouse-fuzz upholstery and a million-liter engine, you got it. Go look for it. I don't know from cars."

"Women never learn the important things in life like what kind of car somebody is driving."

"It was black, that's all I know. Do you think this is important?" Koko asked.

"I don't know. Why didn't you tell me before?"

"I didn't know whether to or not. I thought you might get all twisted because I was gumshoeing around and when I thought about it, it all seemed kind of trivial and pointless. Maybe Mrs. Wardell was sending somebody out to get orange juice for breakfast."

"Maybe," said Digger. "And maybe not." He was thinking of Melanie Fox, dark-haired and big-chested.

"All right," Koko said.

"Koko. You did good."

"Thank you. Good night."

He smoked another cigarette before falling asleep.

When he fought his way back to consciousness, it seemed as if he'd been sleeping only for five minutes. But the sun was up, streaming into the room through the threadbare curtains. Why did he wake up? The telephone. The telephone was ringing.

"Hello," Digger said. He glanced at Koko. She slept on blissfully, unaware of telephones or the world waiting outside to annoy him. How a woman could sleep like that knowing that Cora and the two kids were even now steaming toward Fort Lauderdale was beyond him.

"Is this Burroughs?" a male voice demanded.

"Yeah."

"This is Lieutenant Mannion at headquarters. I'll have a car there for you in five minutes. I want to talk to you."

"This early? I'm warning you. I'm not charming this early."

"I don't want charm, I want information. Five minutes, the car'll be in front."

"Make it ten so I can brush my teeth."

"Ten."

"What's this all about?" Digger asked.

"Ten minutes," Mannion said. "Be ready."

Lieutenant Marvin Mannion looked as if he had been up all night. There were deep bags under his eyes, and a faint stubble was showing around his jowls.

"Sit down there," he growled as Digger entered his office. "Do you know a Randy Batchelor?"

Digger sat down.

"What's this all about?"

"I'll ask the questions," Mannion said.

"Good. You answer them, too."

"I can arrest you, you know."

"And I can get sprung in three minutes and you can hold your hand on your ass waiting for answers. What do you think insurance companies do, anyway, with all the money we steal from fender repair swindles? We hire smart lawyers. I'll be out of here in a flash, so listen, I haven't had any coffee and I haven't had much sleep and spending my morning with you isn't high on my list of must-dos, so why don't we be civil and you tell me what this is all about and I'll tell you anything I know."

Mannion sipped some coffee from a Styrofoam

container as he thought the offer over, then pushed the coffee over toward Digger.

"Here. You can have some of my coffee. All right, Batchelor's dead. You know, you're a brazen bastard."

"Not another plane crash," Digger said.

"Different kind of crash. A bullet crashed into his head."

"Shit," Digger said.

"Where were you last night?"

"In my room at the motel."

"Can you prove it?"

"I had a witness from all day up until about eight o'clock. And then from about eleven o'clock on."

"From eight to eleven, you've got no witness," Mannion said.

"At eight-thirty, I got a phone call in my room. That puts me there then. Then I was playing tapes and making a tape recording. No proof of that. When was Batchelor killed?"

"We don't have a report yet. Sometime between last night and early this morning. You had an argument with him yesterday?"

"An argument?"

"Burroughs, maybe you're dumb but you're not deaf. An argument."

"Oh. It wasn't really an argument. I was out at Interworld Airways, nosing around about this accident. He was there. He came out to talk to me in the parking lot."

"What'd you talk about? Witnesses said it looked like you were arguing."

"Hell hath no fury," Digger said. "The girl who told you that, Jane, was wrong. She's just pissed at me because my girlfriend is prettier than she is. We weren't arguing. I was trying to find out why that plane went down. I told him that I thought he might be involved. He denied it. I thought he might know something but I couldn't get him to talk."

"Why'd you think he might know something?"

"He seemed ready to say something," Digger said. "That and the way he conveniently got sick and got off the plane just before it took off. His little mustache. I didn't like his looks. I think he pushed dope."

"You didn't like his looks so you suspected him?"

"Yeah. That's the way it generally works," Digger said.

"Why'd you think he pushed dope?"

"I was at a party. He was handing out coke like jelly beans."

"Where was the party?"

"I don't know," Digger said. "Some big old house. Melanie Fox would know. She's the stewardess that flew with him a lot."

"I know who she is," Mannion said. "You didn't kill him?"

"No. I was just thinking, Lieutenant. I was making a tape recording last night in my room and I had the TV on. It was a ballgame. The background noise on the tape would be the game. That'd fix the time I was in the room."

Mannion nodded briefly. He seemed unhappy about Digger having an alibi.

"Do you have any idea who might want to kill him?"

"I don't know," Digger said. "If he was doing drugs, who knows? If there was something phony about the plane crash, well, then, that's something different. Maybe somebody who had something to do with that, might have had something to do with Batchelor's death."

"What about the plane crash?" Mannion asked, his voice hardening with suspicion. "You haven't turned up anything yet, have you?"

"Nothing yet but I'm still looking. Where was he killed?"

"At the Oedipus Motel."

"Maybe some chickie shot him 'cause he couldn't get it up."

Mannion shrugged. "If that's a reason, my wife would go for my lungs twice a week," he said.

"Who rented the room at the motel?" Digger asked.

"Some woman. Mary Grissom. Dark hair, sunglasses. You know her?"

"No."

"She paid cash. She gave an out-of-state license plate but we checked and it's a phony. Goddamit, Burroughs, why the hell aren't you the murderer so I could close this up and get a night's sleep?"

"Sorry, Lieutenant, I do my best to please but that's above and beyond. How'd you find me, anyway?"

"Coley out there. Don't look shocked. I knew he was doing some work for you. He told me about it. I thought it was all right if you were going to find out something we didn't know about that plane crash."

"So far all I've done is eat up my boss's money."

"I guessed as much. Okay, you can get out of here, but don't leave town without checking with me."

"I will." Digger got up from the hardbacked chair. "Anybody see this Mary Grissom's car?"

"No. She described it on the application as a white Ford."

Digger walked to the door.

"One last thing, Burroughs."

"Yes."

"A woman was in here yesterday with some lunatic story about Interpol and the Bermuda Triangle. Said some guy from Interpol came and took a letter from her and put a guard on her house. She wanted to know if it was safe to go out. The letter had something to do with one of the crash victims."

Digger laughed. "You really get the half-decks in your business, Lieutenant. I didn't look. Was it a full moon yesterday?"

"It's a full moon everyday in this business. Don't leave town."

"No, sir. I couldn't. My ex-wife and children are coming to visit."

Digger took a cab to Melanie Fox's apartment but she did not answer the bell. When Digger insisted on the doorbell, the upstairs resident of the two-family house finally came to the front door.

"You really know how to ring a bell, don't you?" the woman said. She had a long straight nose, framed by two bulbous cheeks. Her face was blotched red and her hair looked as if it had almost rusted away.

"Sorry to disturb you. I'm looking for Melanie."

"Who are you?"

"A friend of hers. Elmo Lincoln. I was checking out some insurance matters for her."

"Well, you'll have to wait. She went away. Said she had to visit her folks."

"When'd she leave?"

"Yesterday afternoon. She said she'd be a couple of days. Asked me to watch the apartment."

She stopped as if suddenly realizing that Digger might be the advance man for a gang of burglars who specialized in cheap furniture. "I've got my Doberman running around down there every night," she warned.

"I'll be sure to wait until she gets home," Digger said. "Thank you very much." He turned to go, then stopped.

"By the way, she asked me to look into car insurance for her. Do you know what kind of car she has?"

"A Buick, '79 or '80."

"What color is it?"

"Black."

"Thank you."

Digger had kept the cabdriver waiting and he next directed him to Trini Donnelly's house.

He told the cab to wait again and walked to the house. The two sociopaths were nowhere in sight, but Trini was standing behind the screen door, looking at him as he came up the steps.

"What do you want?"

"I've got a question," he said.

"Send it to Dear Abby. My answers are all used up."

"Trini, it's important."

She had seemed ready to slam the inside door but she hesitated briefly.

"Why didn't you tell me your husband was sick?"

"I told you, he stopped drinking," she said.

"I'm not talking about drinking."

"Then I don't know what you're talking about," she said.

"Cancer. Terminal cancer."

"Oh, my god."

"You didn't know?" Digger asked.

"Go away. Please go away."

Digger said, "Will you be all right?"

"Just go," she said. She closed the door. Digger

stood there for a moment. From inside, he heard sobbing.

Koko was in the room, playing the tapes Digger had left in the dresser drawer. She took the ear plug out of her ear.

"Where'd you get the tape player?" he asked.

"I went out and bought it. It's a cheapo but I didn't know how late you'd be and I thought maybe listening would help some."

"Did it?"

"I don't know. Where were you?"

"Police headquarters, by special request. They found Batchelor murdered this morning. They don't know who did it."

"What'd they call you in for? You're not a suspect, are you?" Koko asked.

"No, I don't think so. The lieutenant just doesn't like me and he dragged me in on general principles."

"How was he killed?"

"Bullet in the head while he was lying on the bed, fully clothed in Room 17 of the Oedipus Motel. That's some motherless name for a motel."

"Digger, that's where I lost that cowlet last night in the black car. At that intersection. I remember thinking what a stupid name for a motel."

"That's interesting because the room was rented by a woman with black hair and sunglasses. Just like you saw. But her name was phony and the car description was a phony," Digger said. "Tell me about the tapes."

"I'm sorry, Digger, but I don't want to talk about it. You know I think differently from you."

"I know. You like to stick raw material in your head and forget about it and let it percolate around until answers jump out in a flash of insight," he said.

"Right. And you like to worry things to death like

a puppy with a bone, never letting go, never letting it out of sight, never letting it loose until you bite it in half."

"My way's better," Digger said.

"For you it is. That's because you have an antic mind and if you don't keep after something, you're liable to forget it. Hell, sometimes you can't even remember your own name."

"I remember important things," Digger said. "Like right now, Gorilla Monsoon and What's-his-name and the girl may be in Georgia. Minute by minute, the distance is closing between us and them. Do you think you might stick that information in the back of your brain and tell it to hurry?"

"You can't hurry genius," Koko said.

"Okay, genius. But a couple of other factors for you to think about. Melanie Fox, our dark-haired stewardess with the substantial chest, is out of town. Her landlady said she left yesterday afternoon but she might have left later than that or she might still be in town for all we know. She has a black car. A Buick. That help?"

"I don't know cars," Koko said.

"Added piece of information number two. I don't think Trini Donnelly knew her husband had cancer."

"Okay. About those tapes of yours," she said.

"Yeah?"

"Do you have to hit on every woman you talk to? You're really awful, you know. And the things you said about me, did you mean them?"

"I meant the good ones; the other ones I said in a fit of horny pique. And as far as hitting, the fastest way to a woman's mind is through her pubis. Get them tingling, they'll tell you anything."

"You don't really believe that, do you?" she asked.

"Of course I do," Digger said. He took off his

186

jacket. "Time to get out of this hot tape recorder and into a cold vodka. Who the hell could live in Florida year round?"

"Dig, we live in Las Vegas."

"Yeah, but we don't pretend it's not miserable there. People around here make believe they like this weather."

He stripped off his clothes and peeled off the tape that held the recorder wires to his side, and went to take a shower. He stood for a long time under the cold water, then dried himself, put on fresh underwear and came out to the main room of the motel.

Koko was in bed, under a sheet.

Digger went back into the bathroom, and poured the last drops of vodka from the bottle in the toilet tank. He sat in the living room chair. The wheezing air conditioner squirted a trickle of cool air into the room.

He sipped the cool vodka and saw Koko looking at him.

"Come on over here and feel me up a little," she said.

"I knew if I waited long enough, you'd weaken."

"I'm just taking pity on you, you sex-starved, miserable creep. Before you turn gay in desperation."

"Okay. Well, all right," Digger said. He carried his glass over to the bed.

"I've got it," Koko said.

Digger talked softly into her ear. "Twenty seconds more and I'll have it, too."

"Stop screwing around. This is important."

"It can't wait twenty seconds?" Digger asked.

"That's why you'll never amount to anything. Your mind is ruled by your groin, just like you complain about women for," she said.

"That's right," Digger agreed.

"All right," Koko said with a sigh. "Make love as long as you want. It'll wait. Meanwhile, Madame LeFarge and the two demons are drawing closer, closer, closer. I can feel their hot breath even now crossing the Alabama line."

"We'll make a deal," Digger said.

"What?"

"Give me twenty seconds more."

"Okay. Twenty, nineteen, eighteen, seventeen, sixteen, fifteen, fourteen, thirteen, twelve, eleven, ten, nine, eight, seven, six, five, four, three, two, one. You done yet, Ace?"

"I am now," Digger said.

Chapter Twenty-Three

Digger looked around carefully before he entered the parking lot behind Damien Wardell's parsonage.

He had a long coat hanger hidden inside the sleeve of his jacket. The small lot was dark and quiet. Behind him, from inside the tent, he could hear the sounds of people milling around as the crowds arrived for the evening service. There were five cars parked in the lot where he had parked two days before. Two were white, one was yellow, another was maroon, and the last was black.

Crouching between two cars, he looked around again. There was no sign of anybody. He felt his stomach churning; he was never bothered by a little creative fraud but simple burglary was uncomfortable, particularly if he should happen to get caught and be put in the clutches of Lieutenant Mannion of Lauderdale's finest.

The two dark-colored cars were parked next to each other. Crouching, Digger used a pocketknife to force an opening between the vent window and the main passenger window. Then he slipped the coat hanger through the rubber molding between the windows and twisted it around. It took him five minutes to get the hanger hooked over the door button and to lift it with a quick yank.

He turned to the black car behind him, and swore softly. The car was a newer model and did not have traditional door lock buttons; the locks instead being built into the handles under the passenger's arm-rests.

"Dammit," he hissed. He chewed his lip and turned back to the maroon car. Maybe he'd get lucky. The parking lot was still deserted and he checked the windows of Wardell's parsonage to make sure no one was peering out, watching him. He saw no one, so he opened the car door quickly, slid into the passenger seat, and pulled the door quietly closed behind him.

He took a small penlight flash from his pocket and flicked it on holding it close to the vinyl fabric of the seats, so it would give as little spillover light as possible.

He found what he was looking for on the driver's headrest. He picked it up carefully and placed it in a plain white envelope which he stuck inside his jacket pocket. He breathed a deep sigh of relief as he turned off the flashlight, then waited a few minutes to accustom his eyes again to the dark. When he saw no one in the parking lot, he snuck out of the car, locking the door behind him and shutting it quietly.

He stayed in the shadows, away from the glare of the high overhead lights, and moved quickly back toward the tent, mingling with the arriving crowd, then walked through the parking lot, across the street and to his car which was parked in a restaurant lot around the corner.

"The car was maroon," Digger said. "You said it was black."

"I figured it out after you left," Koko said. "It's that funny green light they use for street lamps."

"Mercury vapor," Digger said.

"Right. It makes red things look black. That's why I thought it was a black car. Did you find anything?"

"One black hair coming up," Digger said. He extracted the small envelope from his pocket and gave it to her. She opened it and hunched herself over the small table under the direct light of the lamp. She removed the strand of hair Digger had found on the seat and placed it atop the white envelope. She looked at it carefully, then picked it up between thumb and forefinger. She ran the nails of her thumb and middle finger on the other hand down the length of the hair. It crinkled up into a tight little curl.

"It's not hair, Digger. It's plastic. From a wig."

"Dammit, you Japanese broads are smart."

"Sexy, too."

"Smart anyway."

Chapter Twenty-Four

The heat had broken. Teaspoon-sized drops of rain fell on the city and changed it in minutes from tropical garden to quagmire marsh.

Cars crawled down the streets, trying to skirt the foot-deep pits of water, piling up in the gutters faster than the storm sewers could carry it off. The dirt parking lot outside the Wardell mission tent, The Church of the Unvarnished Truth, was a wading pool of mud and Digger felt his car sink down as he slowed up and turned in from the street. He pressed down heavily on the gas pedal and muscled the car to the far end of the lot, nearest the main entrance to the tent.

When he stepped from the auto, he felt himself sink into the ooze, up over his shoes, his socks soaking up the water from the mud.

The flap door of the tent was closed, fastened with a rope through grommets on the inside. Digger reached through the narrow slit and with his penknife sawed away a section of rope. Then he pulled on the flap and the split rope slid loosely through the grommets and he stepped inside. He pulled the flap closed behind him, then used his penlight flash to find his way down the aisle to the raised platform that served as a stage. The lighting control panel was in a sealed box on the right-hand rear corner of the stage. The box was not locked and Digger opened it and found a switch neatly labeled "Main Lights." He pulled up the switch and the overhead lights flared on in the tent.

He carefully closed the box and walked across the stage, then climbed up across the rows of bleacher seats until he found a spot halfway up the bank of bleachers, where he sat to wait.

He hoped that this would wrap it up. He wanted to leave Fort Lauderdale. It wasn't just that the beast with three heads was even now in a car lurching toward him. He just wanted to be home, even if home were a condominium in Las Vegas. The older he got, the less he liked traveling. He wanted to be home, with his records, his Freddy Gardner albums, his old Caruso records, his Jazz at the Philharmonic, his Jeri Southern records. *His* music. *His* liquor cabinet filled with bottle after bottle of Finlandia vodka. *His* house. Where he could find his sneakers. And his favorite books. And his personal treasures. The Dali drawing. The jaws of a shark he had once caught at Montauk. His stuffed piranha. His sliced geode paperweight, which was perfectly functional, except he never kept papers and never had anything to put under it. Which was okay in *his* house.

With *his* woman?

Not really, Koko would always be her own woman. They might coexist in the same space; they might even someday realize they loved each other like normal people; but she would never belong to him, just as he would never belong to her.

Maybe, someday, she would find someone she wanted to belong to and with a heartbreaking smile, she would kiss Digger on the cheek and tell him, So long, kiddo. Write if you get work. And she'd be gone. And he would be as alone as ever. Crazy and getting crazier.

He put the thoughts out of his mind as he heard footsteps coming down the wooden ramp toward the stage.

It was Candace Wardell. She stepped onto the stage and walked quickly toward the control box. She was ready to toss the switch when it occurred to her to look around. She glanced upward and saw Digger.

He waved gaily at her.

"Who are . . . oh, it's you. Did you turn these on?"

"Yup."

"Why?"

"I don't like sitting in the dark. I even sleep with a night light."

"What are you doing here?"

"Waiting to talk to you."

"Make an appointment," she said.

"Did Batchelor make an appointment?"

"What are you talking about?"

"Oh, a couple of things. Insurance fraud. Mass murder. Killing a blackmailer."

"You're delusional," she said. "I'm going back to the house."

"Go ahead. Turn off the light, if you want," Digger said. "I can talk to the police just as easy as I can talk to you."

Her hand moved toward the light switch, but it hesitated, then withdrew. "All right, if you want to talk, talk. But come down here so we don't have to shout."

Digger walked down over the seats toward the stage. He stopped and sat again in the first row. Candace stared at him. She was a handsome woman, but again he noticed something hard about her. It was the way she was standing on stage; he recognized it as the way her husband often stood as he delivered a punchline in his sermon.

"It must be tough," Digger said, "to marry millions and then find out that it's being frittered away to the church and you've got no control over it." He felt the comfortable whirring of the tape recorder against his right kidney as Mrs. Wardell walked across the stage toward him. She sat on the edge of the stage in front of him, her legs dangling toward the earthen floor. She wore tight blue jeans and a flowered blouse. Digger thought that the woman was pretty and ample, but not really what he would call bosomy.

"A little girl from a little tank town gets a ticket into the big time and then her husband decides to go follow the Lord, sprinkling his money as he goes."

"It'd make a wonderful movie," she said. "Maybe we can get Tuesday Weld to play it."

"She goes along with the act for a while and plays Holy Mother Sister Superior, singing her songs by the numbers and all the time that jazz singer voice wants to get out and she's trying to find a way out. But there isn't any money that can be touched. It's all in that trust. And she can't even get a nickel if she sues for divorce."

"Interesting. First time I've ever been psychoanalyzed without a couch," she said.

"So you look for a way and then you got it. All those losers . . . remember, that's what you called them . . . all those losers who came to dump their troubles on your husband. Who'd miss them if they vanished? Particularly the ones who didn't have friends or family. But how to get something out of it? And then the Lord delivered Steve Donnelly into your hands. I feel sorry for him. He finally had his life straightened out and then he finds out he's going to die. He's going to leave a wife and kids and mortgage and a lot of debts. Insurance? Forget it. With his condition, he couldn't get insurance anywhere. He probably came to talk to your husband about it and you intercepted him and I guess you showed him the way to do it."

Mrs. Wardell was looking at Digger as if he were a particularly hypnotic snake, swaying back and forth in front of her.

"Sure," Digger said. "He could have an accident, and he could have the accident with this plane full of suicidal losers. Drunks, derelicts, the whole pack who wanted to do something for somebody they wronged but who couldn't produce a dime alive and wouldn't be worth a nickel in insurance if they were dead by suicide. But nobody had to know it was suicide. It could be an accident. A fool's flight of people wanting to die."

Mrs. Wardell was swinging her legs back and forth, clicking her heels rhythmically against the wooden stage.

"Donnelly decided to go along with it. There wasn't much wrong with helping people to die who were going to kill themselves anyway. Of course, that didn't include Batchelor and Melanie Fox. So he had to get them off the plane. My guess is that he larded up his coffee with Ipecac or one of those things that makes babies vomit and then left the coffee where Batchelor would be sure to drink it. I'm pretty sure his neighborhood drugstore will remember him buying some."

"You've been a busy man," she said.

"I had to be. I'm expecting unwelcome guests and I have to get out of Lauderdale. Anyway, it worked like a charm. Donnelly takes off, gets his plane off the radar screen, then probably took it so high that the passengers were knocked out for lack of oxygen, then aimed the plane down at the ocean and smashed it to splinters. Meanwhile, all those nice people aboard had filled out insurance applications naming your husband as beneficiary in the event of their death. Well, actually they didn't fill them out. You did. And your helper. That sleazy accountant of yours, what's his name. . . ."

"Jack Thomasen."

"Yeah, that's him. The one that gobbles you with his eyes. I figure him. I figure that when the police go through your house they'll find a list of all the people that the passengers wanted you to take care of paying off. People they owed, families they'd abandoned, anybody who could stop them from leaving life without a clear conscience. And of course you had no idea of ever paying anybody anything."

"Of course," she said in the tone of voice one would use to humor a madman.

"But then things started to go wrong," Digger said. "First there was Mrs. Donnelly threatening to sue. I told you about that and before I was even out of the parking lot, you called her to back her off. I guess something like this. 'Your husband told us here at the church if anything ever happened on this flight, we were to be sure to take care of you and the children. And of course we will.' That's only a guess, but when I tell her that my company will pay the entire face amount of the insurance to her, no matter what, I'm sure she'll tell us exactly what you told her.

"See," Digger said, "the whole thing with Donnelly's insurance was a mistake. I don't know if you or your boyfriend did it . . . the handwriting analysis will tell . . . but you never should have made out a policy for Donnelly. He would know that he couldn't take accident insurance as the pilot, but you were so hungry to get every last buck, that you didn't bother to read the policy. You know, you shouldn't ever lie to an insurance company. We're smarter than owls, more remorseless than athlete's foot."

"I'll keep that in mind next time."

"And then there was getting all those drunks to the airport. You brought them all here first and got them pretty much blotto to begin with. Then you bussed them down there and got them aboard the plane. The stewardess said most of them were juiced. I got to thinking about that. If they were drunk, how'd they fill out the insurance applications at that little machine? They couldn't. They were all filled out beforehand. I found one of the policies in the room of one of the guys who died. All neatly filled out by this rumdum who hadn't drawn a sober breath in years. But he forgot to send it in and you just couldn't leave it laying around, or so you thought, so you broke into his place and tried to steal it. But you didn't get it. I did. And the same handwriting, just like all the others.

"Then you pleaded surprise. That was another mistake, saying that you never got the insurance policy dupes. But if the people on that plane had just filled out the policies like normal people, some of them would have sent them to you. Not getting any of them just didn't make any sense."

Digger stood and walked back and forth to stretch his legs. He could feel the mud hardening on his socks and shoes. It felt as if he were wearing lead boots.

"You missed another thing. One of your passengers wrote a letter to be mailed after his death. He told his wife, the wife he had run away from, that she would be hearing about him. Not from him. 'About him.' I missed that the first time I read it. It wasn't some letter from a Jesus freak; it was a good-bye note from somebody who knew he was going to die."

He turned back to Candace. "Anything to say?"

"You're doing so well, why bother?" she said.

"But then there was Randy Batchelor. The first time I talked to him, it hit him. That Steve Donnelly wanted him off that plane for some reason. Then he started to snoop around and he finally figured out what happened. He put the squeeze on you. So you went in your disguise and rented a room in the Oedipus Motel and told him to meet you there. Then during last night's service, you slipped out and put on your black wig . . . I guess we'll find it in the house . . . and went and shot him."

"There were fifteen hundred people here last night," Mrs. Wardell said. "They'll swear I wasn't off that stage for more than fifteen minutes."

"Maybe," Digger said. Something was wrong. He was missing something. What was it? "Stay with me," he said. "You killed Batchelor and then you went back to work."

"An awful lot of conjecture," she said.

"Sure. But when I go to the cops tomorrow, I'll just lay it out for them. I think they'll be able to make something out of it."

"Without a hard piece of evidence?"

"Oh, there's some evidence. The leftover insurance policy. The letter that was never mailed. There's the wig. I found hairs from it on the headrest of your car. The life insurance policy on Donnelly that never should have been taken out. All those records I'm sure you keep inside and the coincidence that everybody on that flight had no next of kin, which is just the way you wanted it. The bribe you offered Mrs. Donnelly. The lie about a plane for more than forty people. I guess the cops'll find the gun in your house, too."

"They won't find the gun." The voice was soft but chilling. Digger turned around from the corner of the stage. Erma was standing there, holding a gun on him. Erma, the secretarial mouse with the big bosom, a very big bosom. Of course, Mrs. Wardell had been off the stage for only a few minutes the night before. She had sent Erma on the killing mission. It had been Erma, her blond hair hidden by a dark wig but her big bosom unmistakable, that Koko followed to the motel corner.

"No?" Digger said mildly.

"No," Erma said. "After I'm finished using it on you, I'll dump it in the ocean."

"That's the gun you used on Batchelor?"

"Yes."

"They'll trace the slugs on ballistics. They'll know Randy and I were killed by the same gun. They find my body here, they're going to start wondering about you people and your connections with all these recent deaths."

For a moment, Erma looked confused. She looked toward Candace and Digger immediately understood their relationship and why Candace had appeared almost masculine in her movements.

"Wimp," she barked. "Are you stupid? Shoot him."

Digger dove behind the corner of the stage, just as a bullet cracked over his head and hit a seat behind him. Scuttering like a crab, he moved down the side of the stage, staying low behind the protection of the wooden platform. Another shot cracked out and wood chips flew over his head.

He found the corner of the stage and dove around it. Above his head, he could hear Candace Wardell running across the stage toward him. Another pair of footsteps were coming along the ground around the stage.

He reached up over his head into the electrical control box and pulled down the light switch. The tent was plunged into darkness.

Digger slammed the lid of the box shut and vaulted up into the bleachers just as a bullet whizzed past him. Crouching low, he ran to the edge of the bleachers, dropped heavily to the ground and ran up the slight earth incline toward the back of the tent.

"Dumb bitch," he heard Candace growl. "Find that goddam switch."

Digger had reached the back of the tent and with his right hand on it as a guide, began to run through the dark toward the lone exit. It was easier now. Even through the heavy canvas fabric, some light filtered and he could see slightly. He suddenly realized that so could the two women and in silhouette, he would be a perfect target against the white fabric.

He dropped to the ground as another bullet cracked off and whistled past his head.

He scurried forward and then the tent lights came on, illuminating the inside of the enclosure like a harsh, white operating room.

His only hope was to stay low behind the bleachers, use them for cover and get to the entrance before the women. Another shot cracked toward him and he knew there was no way he could make it. The two women could run at top speed, while he had to slither slow to stay out of the line of fire. He was dead. He knew it. Dead without being around to welcome his ex-wife and children to Fort Lauderdale.

And then there was a voice.

"All right. Police. Drop it." There was a pause. "I said drop it. Don't even think of it."

Digger never thought he would be happy to hear Lieutenant Mannion's voice. Then he heard Koko's voice. She was running toward him.

"Dig, are you all right?"

He rose slowly as she got to him and threw her arms around him.

"Are you all right?"

"What time is it?" he asked.

Koko said, "I don't know. Eleven-thirty, I guess."

"We've got to get moving," Digger said. "Lady Atilla and the Two Huns will be here any minute."

The police were escorting Mrs. Wardell and Erma, in handcuffs, through the tent door, when Digger asked Mannion, "What got you here?"

"The lady here. She made me come."

Digger turned to Koko. "How'd you know?"

"It was the names, Dig. It was on the tape and I just missed it the first time."

"What do you mean?"

"The blonde was named Erma. But you said that Mrs. Wardell called her Ninde. That's short for Urninde. It's German for lesbian. Then it all made sense. The matching outfits. The different-colored handkerchiefs they wore in their back pockets. They're all gay signals. These two lesbians were flaunting it, sure that nobody in poor, old dumb Fort Lauderdale would notice or catch on."

"I don't know German," Digger said. "You couldn't expect me to figure that out. I'm Irish and Jewish. I don't know German. I thought it was the accountant."

"I'm Japanese and Italian," Koko said. "*I* know German."

"That's because you were all on the same side in World War II," Digger said. "And besides, you're smarter than I am. Now let's get out of here before the Manson family hits town."

"What the hell are you two talking about?" Mannion asked. "What Manson family?"

"Some people we don't want to meet," Digger said. "We just want to get out of here."

"Well, you can't just pick up and leave. You've got to stay around here for a while. Statements, complaints, you've got to be around."

"Then I demand to be held in protective custody," Digger said.

"Fine by me," Mannion said.

"Stop your nonsense," Koko said. "I'll get our things and switch us over to another motel."

"They'll find us," Digger whined. "No matter where we go, they'll search us out. We'll be sleeping some night and we'll hear their claws scratching at the door."

Mannion shook his head. "Well, I don't care what you do. Just make sure you're down at my office in a half hour. Now, I've got to go." He turned to Koko and said, "What are you doing with this guy? He's a nut."

Koko's cream-smooth face opened in a small, shy smile.

"But he's never dull," she said.

After Mannion left, Digger asked Koko, "If we just run, do you think he'll put out an alarm on us?"

"With orders to shoot on sight," she said.

"Shit. Nothing ever goes right for me," Digger said.

They heard a voice over on the other side of

the tent. "What's going on here?" It was Reverend Wardell, in pajamas, rubbing sleep from his eyes. "Oh, it's you, Burroughs. What's going on here?"

"I'll tell you if you promise to pray for me," Digger said.

Chapter Twenty-Five

Frank Stevens, the president of Brokers' Surety Life Insurance Company, clicked his fork against a glass, and said, "A toast."

He raised his champagne glass. Digger, next to him, lifted a glass of vodka. Koko raised a glass of water. Digger's father took his right hand off Koko's knee and hoisted a glass of John Jameson Irish whiskey.

Next to him, Digger's mother put her hand around a red spritzer. Walter Brackler lifted a sweet Rusty Nail.

"To Digger," Stevens said. "Long may he rave."

"That's not funny," Digger said, but he drained his glass of vodka anyway.

"I don't see what's so good about finding out that a lot of people committed suicide," Digger's mother said.

"That's because you're not a stockholder in B.S.L.I., Mrs. Burroughs," said Stevens. He was a tall, white-haired man, elegant in a three-piece blue pin-striped suit.

"If anybody ever dies around you, Sarah, everybody'll know it was suicide," Digger's father said.

"Well, I just don't think it was so important that they had to whisk Julian out of town in protective custody, so that he wasn't there to meet Cora and the children."

"I told them, Mother, how important it was for me to meet my ex-wife and What's-his-name and the girl," Digger said, "but they just wouldn't listen. They had me hiding out in a motel fifteen miles out of town. I didn't even have a telephone. Otherwise, I would have called you so you could tell Cora where to find me." Digger winked at Koko who giggled. Digger's father put his hand back on Koko's knee.

"A good job," Stevens said. "One of the best things I ever did for this company was hire you. Don't you think so, Walter?"

Brackler cleared his throat and said, "Errr, I guess so."

"Don't guess," Stevens said. "Of course it was. Right?"

"Right, Mr. Stevens," Brackler said.

"Of course, he had help," Stevens said. He lifted his glass again. "To Koko."

"I'll drink to that," Digger's father said.

"You'd drink to anything," Digger's mother said.

Koko leaned over to Digger's father and whispered, "Ditch her and I'll meet you in the parking lot later."

"Don't tempt me, girl," he said.

"What'd she say?" Mrs. Burroughs asked. "What'd she say?"

"She said she hopes that you and I are always as happy as we are now," Digger's father said.

"Well, heaven knows *I* try," Mrs. Burroughs said. She looked across the table at her son. "Julian. I spoke to Cora and she said she'll be back the day after tomorrow. She hopes you'll be here to see the children."

Digger snapped his fingers. "Oh, too bad."

"What's too bad?" his mother asked.

"When's she coming back?"

"The day after tomorrow."

"Yeah, what a shame. Koko and I are going back to Las Vegas tomorrow. First thing. Early flight. Too bad."

"Yes," Koko said. "Too bad. I really looked forward to meeting Dig's kids."

"I don't know what their mother would think of that," Mrs. Burroughs said.

"How can the woman think anything about that when she never thinks anything about anything?" Digger asked.

"Koko, take this with you," Stevens said. He handed an envelope across Digger to the young oriental woman. She nodded and put it in her purse.

"What was that?" Digger's mother asked.

"It doesn't concern you, woman," said Digger's father.

"I hate it when people have secrets," said Mrs. Burroughs. She saw her son watching her and said, "Look at you. Mr. Stevens is nice enough to buy you dinner and you don't even wear a suit. Look how nice he dresses and look at you."

"Mother, I'm wearing a jacket and tie. Give me a break, will you?"

"I don't know why you dress like that," she said. "You certainly don't take after me or my family."

Digger reached under his jacket, fiddled with something, then pulled out his small tape recorder and placed it on the table. He pressed a button, the tape whirred for a moment, and he pressed another button. His mother's voice, clarion bright, resounded over the table. "I hate it when people have secrets . . . look at you. Mr. Stevens is nice enough to buy you dinner and you . . ."

"Turn that thing off," Mrs. Burroughs said.

Digger did.

"Why did you record that?" she demanded.

"So I'll always have you with me," Digger said.

In the cab, riding back to their hotel, Digger asked Koko, "What was in the envelope that Frank gave you?"

"Oh. I forgot. Let me see." She fished it out of her purse and tore open the end. "Hey, look at this," she said. "It's a check. With a note. 'Hope this covers your expenses.'"

"How much is it for?"

She leaned against the side window of the cab to illuminate the check under a street light.

"Holy shit," she said. "Five thousand dollars."

"Save it," Digger said.

"What for?"

"You'll need it. The next time, *you're* taking *me* on vacation," he said.

"I'll have to call Cora first and find out where she and the kids would like to go. And your mother, too," Koko said.

"Try Devil's Island," Digger said.